CW01511946

A Friend in the Floorboards

By Stefan Scheuermann

This book is a work of fiction. Any resemblance to actual events or persons, living or dead, is entirely coincidental.

"A Friend in the Floorboards," by Stefan Scheuermann. ISBN 978-1-63868-191-5 (softcover); 978-1-63868-192-2 (hardcover); 978-1-63868-193-9 (eBook).

Published 2025 by Virtualbookworm.com Publishing Inc., P.O. Box 9949, College Station, TX 77842, US. ©2025, Stefan Scheuermann. All rights reserved. No part of this publication may be reproduced, stored in a retrieval system, or transmitted in any form or by any means, electronic, mechanical, recording or otherwise, without the prior written permission of Stefan Scheuermann.

This book is dedicated to my parents, Wanda & Gerard Scheuermann, for lending me the inspiration of their extraordinary childhood experiences.

CONTENTS

Chapter One:
In the Familiar Arms of Strangers

CECILE DIDN'T BELIEVE IN GHOSTS. She had never had visions she couldn't explain. She went to church every Sunday and wholeheartedly believed what the priest told her — God lives in Heaven, keeping an ever-watchful eye on us all. We live and we die. The good go to Heaven and the bad go to Hell. They do not linger and haunt old Cajun farmhouses in the heart of Louisiana. Cecile knew this, and it was all she needed to know to go about her days as she should, to attend her Catholic school as a good little twelve-year-old Catholic girl, in her Catholic community, in the city of New Orleans, Louisiana in 1958.

She was a city girl throughout, with a very different upbringing than her mother, Julia. Like Julia, Cecile was born in Moreauville, Louisiana, in Avoyelles Parish. When she was only six, her mother and father moved to New Orleans, taking her from the small Cajun farming community her ancestors had founded.

By the time she was twelve, what remained of Cecile's rural Louisiana culture existed only in upheld but diluted traditions, and stories told vividly by her mother. Her father, Adam Hecker, wasn't Cajun. He came from a line of respectable Louisiana Germans. He had a very thin connection to Moreauville. Like the four generations of Heckers before him, he had been raised in New Orleans. As a senior in high school, he moved with his parents to Moreauville, where he met Julia Lemoine. Adam and Julia were married two years later.

To Cecile, it was all so long ago and so very far away. They had visited Moreauville only three times in the six years since moving to the city. The lives of her grandparents, of her Cajun aunts, uncles, and cousins, were like stories in bizarre tales, to be read at the library, not lived by real people, by real relatives. That all changed that spring in 1958 when Cecile's grandfather died and her grandmother was left to run the farm alone. Cecile was almost thirteen years old.

Paulina Lemoine was a remarkable woman, strong as an ox, strong and capable, yet womanly and motherly. She wielded a hoe and a whisk, a shovel and a book, with equal proficiency. She carried the title, Mema, and there was no more honored title to carry. But her husband had long been the pillar to which she was anchored. He had been a quiet man, but one with admirable skills in everything he put his hand to. Capable as she was, Cecile's grandmother could not run the farm alone.

The funeral was Cecile's first visit to Moreauville in two years. Paulina's small, two-bedroom farmhouse became the coziest bed & breakfast south of Alexandria. The quarters were tight, and the cousins who slept on the floor beside Cecile had faces and names she hardly remembered. It was the longest she had spent with her Cajun cousins since she was six. But they all shared those same striking facial features that branded them as members of the same family, features prominent in Cecile. The eyes, the mouth, the button nose were all strong genetic markings

2

that guaranteed Cecile a familial hug from everyone in the community.

As familiar as her cousins looked, they acted bizarrely. They were an unaccountable blend of traditional formality and rural intimacy. Their conversations were a patchwork quilt of French and English, and words they seemed to make up on the spot. It was all strange. It was all foreign. It was all delightful!

They were there for a funeral, and nobody could forget it. The air was mournful, but it was a Cajun sort of mournfulness, with stories told through giggling tears, and much, much more laughing than crying. By the time they all awoke on the morning of the funeral, Cecile felt like a different colored thread on the same embroidery as her cousins — different than those around her, but stitched tightly and irrevocably to the same canvas, a unique but necessary part of an exotic work of art.

An extravagance of food was served almost hourly as more relatives arrived. Cecile tried briefly to imagine all that food coming off the same little stove in her Mema's kitchen. Separating the kitchen and living room was an old-style swinging door. Cecile imagined what Biblical magic was happening on the other side of it. She didn't consider it long. It was enough for her that the food *did* come, and even though some of the foods were new and unusual to her, like her cousins, it was all familiar in some deeply rooted way.

The heat of the Louisiana summer was still a full month away. The air smelled like a country spring. A breeze blew. It would have been perfectly comfortable if not for the excessive funeral clothing. Cecile wore a dress with a many-layered skirt and a tight bodice. The dress would have kept her warm on the North Pole, or so she lamented to her father. She wished herself there several times during the crowded drive from Paulina's house, along the Bayou Des Glaises, to St. Peter Catholic Church in Bordelonville.

Inside the church, it was even hotter. The church had been built for much smaller gatherings, for the local congregation, without consideration for the occasional wedding or funeral that would cram together sweaty hips and shoulders. The service may have lasted for an hour or four hours. To Cecile, it was a miserable eternity, that is, until her aunts, uncles, and cousins began to speak.

One at a time, they came to the front and told stories of the departed. It was a vocal biography filled with thrilling tales, of comedy and tragedy, and of hardships that seemed to come straight from the Old Testament. Cecile loved living in the city, but while she listened to her relatives speak of their shared experiences of her grandfather, she was jealous. She envied every story told, stories that didn't include her, her mother, or her father. For the first time in her life, she wished she had spent more time in Moreauville. While she listened in delightful regret, nothing so petty as running sweat, tight bodices, or cramped quarters could have affected her.

As her family had driven from New Orleans to Moreauville, Cecile couldn't picture her grandfather's face with any more detail than the portraits hanging in their hallway. By the time the funeral service ended and the casket was hoisted for the march to the cemetery behind the church, she would have given anything waiting for her in New Orleans for one chance to see him smile, hear his voice and his laugh, and squeeze him with the sort of embrace that tells an old man that his granddaughter loves him. In absolute contrast to her feelings as they drove out of the city, she *wanted* to be in "the country", and the thought of leaving and returning to the numb distance of her life in the city strained her heart severely.

After the burial, the old farmhouse became a more lively place than anywhere in the grand old city. There was

4

no regret among *that* crowd, none that Cecile could see. They were happy. More stories flowed from lips, bounced jovially from the walls, and were consumed by ravenous ears. It would have been chaotic if not for the strong sense of rightness, of love and loyalty. Cecile was held, hugged, and kissed more times than she had been in the previous two years combined. She didn't want it to end, and it didn't, even when the sun went down or when the first brush of dawn blushed the horizon above the newly planted fields.

By the time the sky wore the full brightness of day, the relatives began to trickle out. Each departure was a trove of affection. If each hug was a dime and each kiss a dollar, by the time she, her parents, and her grandmother were the only ones left in the house, Cecile could have bought the entire state of Louisiana. Her heart and her stomach had been stuffed in equal proportion, and she fell asleep on the living room couch with the murmurs of her mother and grandmother softly serenading her from the kitchen.

As I mentioned at the beginning, Cecile didn't believe in ghosts, but she dreamed of one that day. She dreamed of her grandfather. He was a pale and smoky apparition, but not frightening. She tried to hug him, but her arms passed through, so she sat and listened to him. He told her stories of the family, stories of Avoyelles Parish and the families that built it. He introduced her to many other specters, each connected to the family in some way. As he did, his figure became less ghostly, more substantial. Finally, she built the courage to reach for him. To her terrified delight, he was solid, warm, and very much alive. She leaped into his embrace. He hoisted her into his arms and began to walk with her. She awoke in the arms of her father, as he carried her to Paulina's bedroom and laid her lovingly on the bed.

Cecile pretended to still sleep, but she could not. The images of the ghosts in her dream were projected vividly on her inner eye, and whether her eyes were open or shut, there they were. She laid still for several minutes after her father left the room, hoping to sleep yet afraid to let go of the feeling inside of her. She got up and walked light-headed from the bedroom. She had ghosts on her mind, so she was only moderately shocked when she walked into the living room and saw half of a shadowy phantom on the floor in front of her.

There was a green haze around it. It was facing away from her. It had no legs, no hips. It was a human figure, well, half of a human figure. Its lower half was missing. There it sat from the waist up, propped erect on the hardwood floor beside the couch where she had fallen asleep. Although it appeared severed in half, it showed no signs of distress, not like the angry, mutilated ghosts from the horror stories. In fact, it laughed. In the mere seconds Cecile viewed it, the emerald-green haze around it lightened, revealing the clear back of a boy. The figure began to turn. Cecile gasped, and in that very instant, it was gone. The living room was just as it had been all day.

Assuming herself still half-asleep in a lingering dream, she rubbed her eyes, giggled at her own silliness, and whispered quietly, "Hmm, I have ghosts on the mind."

It was no wonder to her that the figures from her dream projected themselves onto her waking vision. She had stayed up through the previous day and night, hearing tales of departed relatives, sipping occasionally from the adult bowl of punch. It didn't distress her, nor frighten her of the old house. It endeared Moreauville, the old farmhouse, and the whole family to her, and made all the sadder her impending return to the city.

In the country, lunch was the largest meal of the day. They called it dinner. And breakfast was not relegated to the mornings. Fried eggs, thick slices of ham, grits, all things Cecile ate regularly in New Orleans, but only in the morning, were often served late in the evening. Combined with her distorted sleeping schedule, she couldn't tell what time of day it was by the food being served at the table. Dawn and dusk were experienced much the same.

In the evening, two days after the funeral, Cecile's grits and eggs were accompanied by delightful conversation. Her parents were negotiating regular visits with Paulina. Paulina had a melodic way of talking. Each sentence seemed to send her up and down a full scale of notes. This was especially the case when she was emotional or trying to convince someone to agree to something.

She traveled the scales three times as she said, "Most of the year I am well enough on my own, but cher, planting and harvest is too much. That's when I'm gunna need ya.'"

Cecile's mother rebutted, "But that's three weeks at a time, twice a year. Can't you hire someone?"

Scraping mid-baritone then swinging up to tickle the heights of soprano, Paulina answered, "Planting time is planting time for everyone. Same with harvest. Who can I hire? No cher, this is a *family* farm. This is *your* farm."

Paulina began to describe Julia's birth for the fourth time in the previous two days. This time, she couldn't get beyond the onset of labor pains before being interrupted.

Julia reminded her, "Adam can't come for six weeks a year. We were lucky to have him for Daddy's funeral. And how much good would I be for you alone?"

"You?" Paulina exclaimed at three times the necessary volume, "All I need are these big muscles here."

She turned to Cecile, winked, and squeezed her thin arm. Julia and Adam laughed, but stopped when they saw their daughter's face. To Cecile, it was no laughing matter. As Paulina said, she was strong. She could help. She would have offered much more to come to Moreauville twice a year and spend three full weeks at a time with her Mema, hearing vibrant stories and eating her cooking.

"I can help," she argued, "I can plant seeds. I carry five big books in my bookbag for eight blocks to school."

Cecile's indignation was impossible to misinterpret, and the parents set immediately to compliment her. Paulina just smiled. She had planted a different sort of seed that day, and nobody was better at it. Before the grits stopped steaming, it was agreed. Julia and Cecile would come for planting and harvest. Adam would join when he could.

Chapter Two:
The Inept Farmhand

THE EVENTS OF THE FUNERAL were extraordinary in the life of the young girl, but time brushes quickly and abrasively against us, causing calluses on our hearts. A sort of spiritual amnesia settled over Cecile's heart. She didn't forget the funeral. Her memory was not *so* crusted over, but the intensity of *feelings* she felt in Moreauville became less lively with every passing week. She finished the school year, began her summer, turned thirteen, played with her friends, and built new, fun memories. Stories of the dead, dreams of ghosts, even her grandmother's cooking had to find a quiet place in the back corners of her thoughts.

The next school year began, and Cecile's attention was far from Moreauville. When harvest time came, her eagerness to return to the country was not as powerful as her reluctance to leave had been. It was already several weeks into the new school year, and Cecile was knee-deep in all the things a new school year brings. It would be an exaggeration to say that she dreaded going back to her Mema's house, but she had friends and plans that she was not too keen to exchange for long, sweaty, laborious days on a farm.

Adam had a few days to spare, so he drove his wife and daughter to Moreauville. A family road trip was always special. Getting away as a family was a treasure. To Cecile, it always felt like a rolling picnic, with snacks and treats she never had at home, and conversation, the length and subjects of which were never heard at their dinner table. It was the perfect three-hour transition from one world into a very different one. By the time they entered Avoyelles Parish, the city and everything in it was fully behind them.

Near the end of the drive, conversations had gone quiet. Cecile was half-asleep in the back seat, riding on free, unguided images, with her heavy eyelids barely open, until they turned off the highway. They were close, and excitement surged through her like a drug. This was the part of the drive she observed closely. The familiar levee rose high to her right, holding back the Mighty Mississippi from the rich farmland to her left. They turned away from the Mississippi and crossed the Atchafalaya River.

On the other side of the bridge was the tiny town of Simmesport. It was a little river port community, with less activity than a single block of the French Quarter in New Orleans. But to the farming families of Avoyelles Parish, Simmesport was a metropolis. It was the commercial hub and the trade port for the area's farming families. Although you would drive through it without noticing if you happened upon a series of four or five consecutive, poorly-timed sneezes, it held excitement for the communities that surrounded it, for it was the place to buy exciting new things that came down the river, and to meet an occasional stranger.

It wasn't the stores in Simmesport that Cecile looked for, but beyond, to the curving road along the bayou, the turn off of the road, onto Paulina's farm. The change from pavement to dirt and the sound of the tires rolling over the cattle guard struck a deep chord of warm memories. Immediately past it was the gate. Adam stopped the car, as he had so many times before, opened the gate, drove through, got out again, and closed the gate. It was more of a ritual than a duty. It signified the outside world being closed off behind them.

There were no cell phones back then to call and say, "We're here." There was the sound of the cattle guard and the squeak of the gate, and no sooner did the car come to a final stop than Paulina made her appearance on the front porch, with a smile warmer than the Louisiana air and arms stretched out wider than the Mighty Mississippi.

The main meals of the day were behind them, but that was no reason for an empty stove when family arrives, not in a Cajun home. Bags and suitcases were dropped right inside. Hugs, kisses, and the traditional compliments were paid at the door, then it was off to the washroom and then the table.

It was a well-established fact that food would be served upon arrival, and almost continuously during the visit, yet Paulina always felt the need to excuse the embarrassment-of-riches coming from her kitchen with the same comment she used for years.

She pinched Adam's shoulder like a doctor examining a patient, took a step back, glared at him from top to bottom, then said, "Cawww cher, you're all the time so skinny! Julia Honey, put on some rice."

The rice was already on the counter, and the rice pot was already on the stove. Beside it was the largest cooking vessel on their side of Baton Rouge. Cecile could have bathed in it. In fact, she had, many times during her earliest years. That evening, there was no child in it, but enough gumbo to serve a grand party.

Paulina's table was a similar shape to the table at Cecile's home. It was of a similar color, of comparable dimensions. Physically, it was more or less the same, but a Cajun dinner table is not known for its peculiar dimensions. It's the *spirit* of the table and those who surround it that make it special among all tables in the nation. A seat at Paulina's table was a place of honor for all who took one up, for each person at a Cajun table is adored, honored like a dignitary, and served the portions of royalty.

By the time the steam from the bowl of okra gumbo in front of her mixed with the smell of freshly baked french bread, Cecile could not imagine being anywhere else. Even the glow of the lightbulbs seemed to treat the air around them differently than in the city. The last time it was all experienced just so was in the spring, and it cordially coaxed those reclusive memories out of the corners of Cecile's heart to compete admirably with the pungency of the aromas from the kitchen. A long, hot day of harvesting still awaited her in the morning, but for that special feeling at her Mema's table, Cecile would have paid any price.

After a restless sleep the night before, a long day of driving, a belly full of Paulina's cooking, and such a heavenly atmosphere, Cecile left the supper table hardly able to keep her eyes open. She changed into her pajamas, brushed her teeth, and made her way to the living room couch, which had been made up as a bed. The house bore a different atmosphere than in the spring, without the clamor of chattering cousins.

It wouldn't have mattered anyway. There was a tremendous box fan at the far end of the house. It stood chest-high to Cecile. The fan was powered by an old, squeaky fan belt with rusted gears. From her makeshift bed in the living room, it sounded like the chatter of a small crowd of revelers. An occasional high-pitched squeak would sound out from it, like a child laughing. As she drifted in and out of sleep, Cecile's imagination pulled words and phrases from the ceaseless noises of the fan. The company she imagined was kind and protective, as the fan lulled her into crowded dreams.

She awoke only once in the night. The fan rumbled on, and as she bubbled to the surface of a dream, she sat up, half-expecting to see a crowded living room around her. She opened her eyes and didn't see a crowd, but a single figure, a ghostly figure. It was a young black boy, pure and beautiful of complexion, staring at her with a look of terrified astonishment.

She saw him clearly, yet clearly through him. Cecile could see the floor and wall behind him, as if through a heavy fog. The air around him wavered like the air above a flame, but with a greenish hue. It was not the fact that she could see through him, nor his terrified expression or the ghostly vapors that surrounded him that sent chills across Cecile's entire body. The boy was only half a boy. He had no legs, no hips. He stood on the floor upon his waist, sticking up from the dark floorboards like a candle. She had all but forgotten the dream-like figure she had seen in the spring, but as she stared at the image in front of her, the memory rushed onto her vividly. It was undoubtedly the same boy.

Cecile tried to scream, but only a wave of voiceless air came from her mouth. She scooted quickly to squat on the far arm of the couch. When she raised her eyes again to the center of the floor, the boy was gone. The greenish vapors remained for a flash of a second longer, then faded away, and the living room was as it had been.

Cecile shook in fear, but she didn't call out for her family for fear of recalling the ghostly boy. After a breathless minute of staring wide-eyed at the floor, she released her held breath in the form of a slowly surfacing whimper. She didn't remember falling back to sleep, but awoke alone in the guest bed, where her mother and father had slept.

It was early in the morning, and the faintest pink of dawn colored the window. The room was empty, and the house seemed empty, except for a muted bustle that seemed to come from the living room. The living room! The full terror of her experience with the ghostly boy flooded back into her heart. She remained in bed for another twenty minutes, listening to the soft noise beyond, imagining what sort of mischief a young ghost with no legs could get into. As she strained her ears harder she knew — it was no half-ghost in the living room she heard, but a living woman in the kitchen, making the sounds of an active cook, and singing a song in French.

Cecile's fear subsided, and she dismounted the bed with confidence. The kitchen was to the right of the living room. To get to it, she would have to walk across the very spot where the ghost's belly stood on the floor. She peered tentatively into the room. Her bedding had already been removed from the couch, and the large, embroidered throw pillows sat where she had slept, like a king and queen on their thrones.

There were no ghosts and no green vapors. The room was excessively normal, and the fears of the night became like lucid memories of a bad dream. Cecile chuckled at herself and turned her attention to the action in the kitchen. There was indeed someone cooking and singing in the kitchen. It was her Great-Aunt Nora. The dishes from a breakfast for four already sat clean and drying. For Paulina, Julia, and Adam, and for Aunt Nora, the day was already well underway. Nora was frying more bacon and eggs for the only one among them not up before dawn.

In a swooping, swinging tone that sounded just like Paulina, Nora turned to Cecile and shouted, "Caawwww, mon ti chérie! You've grown."

Nora had been at the funeral, but among the crowd of nieces, nephews, and grandchildren, Cecile hadn't been singled out for close inspection. Before the funeral, it had been many years. That morning in the kitchen, it was just the two of them, and oh, how Nora's eyes held her with reverent love. Cecile felt adored. She felt elevated.

After a downpour of hugs and kisses, Cecile asked, "When did you get here?"

"Oh, long before you got up."

"Where are my parents? Where's Mema?"

Nora smirked and answered, "Cher, it's harvest. The sun is a late riser at harvest. But don't you worry, child. You will join them soon enough. Now you eat."

Cecile took a chair at the table, and Aunt Nora served her breakfast. Between chews and swallows, Cecile solicited every morsel of information her great-aunt could tell her about the old house and the many people who had called it home.

Were it not harvest, were the visit only a visit, Cecile and Nora would have been content to sit and talk until it was time to eat again. But it *was* harvest, and Julia, Adam, and Paulina were already long at work. When Cecile finished her breakfast, she skipped to the spare room to dress for the day, while Nora cleaned the kitchen and continued the same song she had been singing.

Cecile put on her sun dress and returned to the kitchen. As she put on her shoes, Nora stopped singing and commented, "Poor Celeste used to do the cleaning. Aww Poor Celeste. You know, cher, since she died, I've been coming over and helping my little sister…, Poor Celeste."

Cajuns aren't good at hiding their emotions. They have no desire to. As Nora spoke of "Poor Celeste", her voice cracked, and her eyes welled with tears.

The subject intrigued Cecile, but Poor Celeste would have to wait. Cecile tore out the door, anxious to contribute.

By the time she got out to the cornfield, four large baskets of corn had already been picked and sat at the edge of the wall of stalks. Cecile could hear muffled conversation from within. She called to her mother. Julia came out, grabbed a basket of corn, carried it to the trunk of a large tree, and set it down.

"Sweetie," she instructed, "we need you to shuck and husk the corn."

Whatever subject those muffled conversations covered, Cecile wanted to be part of it, and she protested, "But I want to help you pick."

15

"And you will…, at some point. Right now, we need it shucked and husked. Besides, picking is hard work. Sit here in the shade. That'll be much better."

Cecile wasn't upset long. She looked around her. There were no large buildings, no streetcars or bus stops. She was at the farm in Moreauville, and quite content. She kissed her mother with a smile and sat against the trunk of the tree, with the basket of corn beside her. She grabbed the first ear of corn and wondered about Poor Celeste.

The shucking wasn't so difficult. The husking was much harder. She pulled on the strings of husk, from the top, from the bottom, she even tried using her dress to grab them. They held to the corn like they were scared to let go. About half an hour later, Julia came with another full basket, expecting to replace it for a well-shucked and husked basket beside her daughter. There was Cecile, red-faced with frustration and nearly in tears beside a basket of hairy corn.

Julia mistook the redness for heat exhaustion and sent Cecile inside to cool off and rest. Cecile wasn't sad to be away from the corn, but she was very upset about being so useless to her family. She went inside hoping for the kind words of her great-aunt, but Nora was already gone. She had come, cooked, cleaned the house, and left for her own domestic responsibilities. Cecile was alone.

She fixed herself a glass of water. Plopped on the living room couch, and cried.

The fact is, she *was* overheated. Her head throbbed and ached. But all that evaporated in an instant when a voice called to her, "Little girl, why are you crying?"

Cecile looked to the center of the room and there, rising up from the floorboards, was the same young black boy, legless as before, surrounded by the same greenish vapors. She gasped and dropped her glass of water onto the couch beside her. She didn't cower onto the arm of the couch this time, but leaned slightly forward to gaze at him more directly.

Such an apparition should have terrified her, but there was softness in his voice and such kind concern in his face. Chills didn't fly across her until he added, "Is it because you have died?"

For a flash of a moment, Cecile thought that maybe she *had* died. But the thought left her quickly when she looked around, smelled the signature scents of the farmhouse, and felt the wetness of the spilled water against her hip. Her mortality no longer a question, she swelled with compassion for the poor ghost in front of her.

"I have not died," she told him, "I am real, see?" She slapped herself on the arm a few times to demonstrate her solid nature.

He slapped himself in imitation, then asked her, "If you're not a ghost, how are you floating up there, halfway to the ceiling?"

Cecile looked around her in confusion. She tapped her toes on the floor, then looked up at the high ceiling above her. She asked, "What are you talking about? I'm sitting on the couch."

The boy turned to his left, pointed at an empty wall, and asked, "You mean that couch? You're not there. You're floating in the air."

It became clear to Cecile that the boy couldn't see the couch she sat on. It was invisible to him. Embarrassed, she pulled her feet beneath her and tucked her legs in below the bottom of her dress. The boy giggled and turned away until she was done.

He turned back to her, laughed, and said, "You are a funny ghost. What was your name?"

Rather indignantly, she answered, "My name **IS** Cecile, and I am not a ghost. You're the ghost. Look, you have no lower half. What happened to your legs? Were you chopped in half?"

This time, it was the boy who was confused. He looked down toward the floor then back to Cecile, and said, "Nothing wrong with my legs, see?"

He began to move in circles around the floor, like somebody was pushing his nub of a torso from behind.

Compassion overwhelmed Cecile, and with swelling eyelids, she said to herself, "He thinks he still has legs."

After making a few more circles around the room, the boy spoke, "You're teasing me, aren't you? You really are a funny ghost. My name is Perry, and I work here on this farm."

Cecile began to put the pieces together. "Some accident," she thought, "He must have been a farmhand who died on the farm." She determined to ask Paulina. Surely she would know if a young boy had been cut in half on the farm. It's not the sort of story that fades away with time.

It was a matter for later investigation. She turned her attention to the boy, who was, despite his truncated form, a very nice boy. She remembered her manners and told him, "It is nice to meet you, Perry."

Perry fell forward onto his face, sank beneath the floor, and rose again, as if bowing low to her. He opened his mouth to speak, but disappeared along with his surrounding vapors when Julia walked into the room to check on Cecile. Cecile was startled and reacted more violently than when she first saw Perry.

"Sweetie, are you all right?" Julia asked with motherly concern, "I didn't mean to startle you. It's only me."

"I'm all right. I just..., there was a..."

Cecile stared at the floor where Perry had been, then back to her mother.

"What?" Julia asked, "Did an animal get in the house? A possum? Those are mean little monsters that will attack you as soon as look at you."

"No, no," Cecile assured her, "There was no animal. It was a—"

What could she say? How could she say it? She couldn't tell her mother she had been in conversation with half of a black ghost. Alone in the living room with a black boy would have been even more distressing to her mother than idle chat with the departed. The first would have gotten her grounded for life. The second would have gotten her a trip to the doctor. She looked back to the spot on the floor and was no longer sure any of it was real.

She shook herself vigorously, as if trying to get a hundred bugs off of her, then looked to her mother and said, "I didn't see anything. I was just imagining stories."

"Well," Julia answered satisfied, "We're in the country now, and there's not much time for that." She held an ear of the horribly husked corn in front of her and continued, "Come, I'll show you how to *pick* the corn, but I don't think you'll enjoy it."

Cecile rose, took her mother's hand, and walked with her out of the house.

Chapter Three:
The Phantom Teacher

PICKING THE CORN WAS NOT NEARLY AS FUN as Cecile had imagined. The conversations she had hoped to be part of were mundane, mostly about crops, insects, timetables, and Adam's job. It was very hot among the stalks, much more than under the tree. For the first three-quarters of an hour, Cecile didn't mind the boredom and the heat. Her mind was on the friendly phantom she had met in the living room.

"The poor thing," she said several times to herself, "for him to think that *he* is still alive and *I* am the ghost."

Before the close of an hour in the field, Cecile could think of nothing but the heat and the boredom. Another hour and a half passed this way, picking one ear of corn for every ten picked by her father. When she could bear no more, she excused herself to the tree and another attempt at shucking and husking.

It didn't go any better the second time. But her frustration was brief. Paulina had gone inside shortly after Cecile had left the house. She had changed clothes and begun dinner. By the time the stringy husks seemed the very hands of the devil, Paulina rang the dinner bell. It was shortly after noon, and the cool house awaited with the biggest meal of the day.

Cecile joined her parents, holding hands between them and skipping to the door. She had no conscious thoughts of Perry. That is to say, he was not on the top of her mind. But a strange agitation scratched at her from just beneath.

The dinner was set for a party ten times larger than those present. Serving dishes ran down the center of the long table. There was baked ham, chicken fricassee, and smothered pork chops, green beans cooked with bacon, and "new potatoes", corn on the cob, rice and potatoes, and a tomato-cucumber salad. Paulina was the last to sit down, but she didn't remain seated for long.

There was a knock on the door. Paulina sprang to her feet like a twenty-year-old. A young man and a slightly older woman were escorted to the table. They had come to help with the harvest, but timed their arrival perfectly with the feast before them. They were introduced to Cecile as cousins Alfred and Nicole, but whose cousins and on which side, nobody seemed to care. They were family. Cecile remembered their faces from the funeral. That was enough for her.

Paulina offered them a place at the table. They expected to eat, but even if they hadn't, to refuse would have been a grievous insult, so they took the last two chairs. Paulina's chair sat empty while she circled the table like a buzzard, carefully watching the plates. No sooner was an inch emptied by a bite, than Paulina grabbed a serving dish and refilled it. It was not enough that there was always food on the plates. The plates were always full, as if not a single bite had been taken.

Adam had spent his share of meals at a Cajun table, but he wasn't Cajun, so when he was full, he told her, to which Paulina responded, "Aww, Boo, you don't like it."

Adam replied with a waterfall of compliments, and he accepted yet another helping.

Alfred and Nicole were not the last to come. Two more times there were knocks on the door. Five more cousins joined them. The table was already crowded, but somehow, room was made. The moment another entered the dining room, everyone scooted closer together. Chairs seemed to appear out of nowhere, and the family dinner became a banquet. Eleven diners in total, and Paulina continued to circle the table refilling plates from the serving dishes.

The dinner atmosphere was delightful chaos. Multiple conversations ran simultaneously. Nicole masterfully wove herself out of one, into another, out and back in again. They spoke of the future of the farm, the current situation, and the past. Julia spoke of Poor Celeste, and the fond memories she had of her. On one side of Cecile, a cousin cried heartily while speaking of a "poor" relative, while on her other side, someone laughed at a funny memory being recalled.

It didn't take Cecile long to piece it together — the title "Poor" always preceded the name of someone who had died. Someone spoke of "Jean". Jean was still alive. Someone else spoke of "Poor Gaston." Gaston was dead. This was their code, and cracking it made Cecile feel even more like family.

The mention of departed servants reminded Cecile of Perry, and she mustered the courage to ask her Mema.

"Did you ever have a farmhand?"

"Oh, yes, we've had a few. We had many more when I was a girl. My Papa always had them coming and going."

This line of conversation was not so peculiar as to cease the chaotic blend of simultaneous topics, until Cecile asked, "Were any of them black boys?"

This turned a few heads, then she added, "Did any of them die on the farm, maybe cut in half?"

All conversation stopped. Adam rubbed his temples, with an uncomfortable grimace that may have been due to his daughter's question, or may have been caused by more food stuffed into his stomach than he usually ate in a week.

Everyone stared at Cecile. Julia shook her head and said, "Sweetie, you say the darndest things."

Paulina squinted her eyes and tilted her head in thought, then answered, "Many of them were black, but I never heard of one dying on the farm, and I definitely would remember if someone had been cut in half."

They all laughed and returned to their previous topics. Cecile shrunk in her chair, not from embarrassment, but in deep contemplation. She thought of Perry and wondered if maybe he had lived and died too long ago for anyone at the table to remember. She was determined to see him again and ask him what year it was. Only then could she know when he lived, and when he might have died.

The meal ended. Everyone went out to the fields to continue the work, everyone but Adam, who had to return to the city right after dinner. Only Paulina remained behind to clean, and Cecile, who clung to her hip, as if she could extract long-lost family secrets from that one inch of physical connection. She stared at her Mema, while Paulina piled dishes in the basin.

It suddenly struck her. The answers were not hiding in Paulina's hip, but in the poor, gentle ghost.

"You can go with the others," Cecile declared, "I'll stay here and clean up."

"You sure, ma bonne fille? It's a big mess."

Cecile stood straight to appear taller, as she answered, "I'm a big girl now, see."

Paulina, who was not so very much taller, took a step back to observe her head to toe, and she boasted, "Look at you. You sure have grown. You're a good inch taller than this morning."

They laughed. They hugged. They kissed and laughed some more, then Paulina left for the fields, and Cecile was alone in the house.

She cleaned, as she said she would, but it took her twice as long as it should have. Between each washed dish, between each wipe of the table or counter, she peered into the living room for green vapors. It was just a living room, not a lounge for severed specters.

Cecile finished the cleaning with a few hours still left in the workday. She still felt the need to be useful, but what could she do? She couldn't conquer the corn. Besides, there were plenty of hands on the farm that afternoon. So, she roamed about the house, looking for things to dust or straighten, walking in and out of the living room, straining her eyes to the center of the floor.

Her heart wouldn't allow her from the living room for consecutive minutes, so she settled on a new project, to organize the books on the living room bookshelf. Many of the books were in French, and Cecile's French was limited to the common phrases used in an English-speaking Cajun home. But there were many English classics. There was one little book that caught her attention; a thin, illustrated short-story, a fairly new addition to the family collection. It was *The Canterville Ghost* by Oscar Wilde. Oh, how tyrannically it seized her fancy. Nothing else would be dusted or organized that day. She took the book and settled on the couch.

No sooner did she have her legs folded beneath her than she heard him, "Pssst, Cecile."

The book dropped to her side as if it fell out of existence. What need would she have of a ghost story? She had her very own personal ghost.

Perry looked side to side, like he was trying not to be seen by anyone but Cecile, and he whispered again, "Pssst, Cecile."

"You're acting silly," she said in an excited, booming, *outside* voice, "Why are you whispering? There's nobody else in the house."

Perry gestured toward the kitchen, as if to say, "Look, they're right there."

24

Cecile looked toward the kitchen door. There was nobody there, and she assured him, "Everybody's outside. We're all alone."

"S'il te plaît, Cecile, please. They gunna hear you. Who knows what they'll do? They might try to get rid of you."

A sudden and sinking sense of dread fell over her as she realized he wasn't speaking of *her* people, but of his. She shrank to the smallest possible proportions on the corner of the couch, darting her eyes in all directions, looking for other ghosts, less friendly ghosts.

He continued, "Some folks, you know, they're scared of ghosts. They could call a priest or someone, you know, to force you out. But I'm not scared of ghosts, not ghosts like you."

Cecile's fear left her, and she was determined to convince him that she was not the dead one. With her very next breath, she asked him, "What year is it…, to you?"

"Oh, I see," he answered, "You wanna see which one of us is really here, and which one is from the past. That's a good idea. It's 1909, so you see? I can't be the ghost."

It was a small victory for Cecile, small compared to her compassion. She didn't march triumphantly into her next statement, but with a crack in her voice and sadness in her eyes.

"Perry, it's 1958. I'm so sorry, but you have died."

She began to cry, staring at his face for his reaction. He wasn't scared or sad. He thought she had misspoken.

"You mean 1858," he insisted, "Ghosts come from the past. I know that. And if I'm the ghost, why do I stand on the floor, while you float in the air?"

"No Perry," she said with increasing sadness, "It's 1958."

"But I don't haunt this house," he argued, "I only work here. I've been working on the harvest all day."

She replied, "I was working on the harvest this morning…, well, trying…"

As she thought about her ineptness as a farmhand, she bit down on the inside of her cheeks and winced in shame.

It was Perry's compassion that swelled at her obvious distress. He dropped all thoughts of who was dead and who was alive, and thought only about the feelings of his new friend. He slid toward her and asked, "What's wrong? Don't they let you help?"

"They want me to help, but I'm no good. I couldn't even husk the corn."

"Well, that's *tres difficile* until you learn just how."

They sat in silence staring at each other for a few deep breaths, then he suddenly animated and announced, "I can show you. I do it lots, and I'm good at it. Wait here!"

He slid on his ghostly torso toward the kitchen, then stopped, turned to her, and apologized, "I'm sorry. I shouldn't have said that. Where else would you go?"

He disappeared in a blink, but the green vapors remained in his absence. She obeyed him and sat in place, while thoughts of many subjects crashed into her, fighting for supremacy. Her desire to help her family, the mystery of her new friend, whether to tell anyone about him, *how* to tell anyone about him, all scratched away for the top spot in her head.

The battle in her was brief. Within a minute Perry returned. He had an ear of corn in each hand. Like the boy who held them, they were ghostly. One was thin and dried and already shucked. She knew it right away as feed corn. The other was a plump corn on the cob, in its husk, just like the ones she had struggled with in the morning.

"Watch this," he directed.

She watched as he shucked the corn, leaving the clingy strings of husk. He rubbed the feed corn against it and across it, like a bow on a fiddle. The husks loosened and relinquished. Then with his fingertips, he pulled the husks off easily.

"Here, you try," he invited, as he reached the corn toward her.

She tried to take it from him, but it passed right through her hands like steam.

They both said at the same time, "I'm sorry."

He began, "I almost forgot you're a…," but he cut his thought short.

She completed it for him, "a ghost…, that one of us is a ghost."

They gazed at each other, each feeling a strange combination of compassion and competition.

Perry abruptly turned his head to his right and frantically whispered, "Here they co—"

He disappeared and his accompanying vapors dissipated within a couple of seconds. Perry was gone again, but two things had been accomplished. She knew he was from the past, that he was the ghost, and she knew that she grew quickly to like and trust him. More than that, he seemed to like and trust her.

Chapter Four:
A Child's Ambitions

CECILE AWOKE THE NEXT DAY BEFORE DAWN, excited to put her new knowledge to the test. It didn't occur to her for a moment that Perry and what he taught her might have been no more than the imaginings of a bored girl, that she would rub feed corn across the husk and nothing wonderful would happen. She also didn't consider that she wouldn't be invited to shuck and husk corn after the debacle of the previous day.

She had done a wonderful job cleaning, and Aunt Nora would have gladly relinquished the responsibility. Paulina and Julia praised her for her domestic triumph, but Cecile had no interest in dishes or countertops. She had Perry on her mind, and she wanted only to sit under the tree with a basket of corn.

"But you hated shucking the corn," Julia recalled to her.

"Daddy and the cousins are all gone," Cecile reminded her, "It is only us ladies today. Let me try again. I'll do better. I know I will."

Her declaration came just seconds before the knock on the door. Aunt Nora arrived.

Paulina smirked at Cecile, and told her, "Well, if you are to work with us, you must eat with us and start with us."

She let Nora in. Breakfast was cooked and eaten, and Cecile walked to the cornfield with her mother and Mema. With all of the helping hands the day before, there was almost as much corn waiting in baskets as remained still on the stalks. Julia set Cecile up under the tree as before, with much more corn to shuck. She left her daughter there and joined Paulina, with no reason to believe Cecile's abilities had improved overnight.

Once Julia was back in the field, Cecile hopped up, ran into the barn and fetched an ear of feed corn. She returned to the tree, shucked a cob, and began to fiddle away as Perry had taught her. It worked exactly as she expected. The husks fell off like they were tired of sharing company with the kernels. In less than an hour, she had three baskets of husked corn at her feet, each kernel of each cob as naked as a newborn.

At the end of that hour, Julia and Paulina had finished the picking. They came back to the tree to check on Cecile and enjoy some shade. It is hard to describe Julia's astonishment. After staring open-mouthed for a full twenty seconds, she looked around to see who might have helped. There was nobody else there, only the triumphant Cecile, whose smile set a new personal record for height and width, and whose redness of face was *not* due to frustration or the heat, but the prideful blush of a young Cajun who felt useful to her family.

Julia stuttered, "I don't…, how…, who…?"

Paulina cut her short, saying, "I told you, cher, it's in her blood. She may live in the city, but she was born on this farm. We just had to flush the city out of her with some of her Mema's cooking."

Cecile and Paulina laughed, while Julia stood in silent amazement.

Paulina gestured for Cecile to come to her, saying, "Aww, ti cher, that's my gentille fille."

As Cecile reached her embrace, Paulina pulled Julia into her and held them both together. When the group hug had run its course, Cecile pulled away, excited to show them what she had learned, but she stopped short of speaking. Paulina had attributed her success to her blood, to her connection to the family. Cecile didn't want to lose that by admitting she learned it from someone else, and not just someone, but a young black ghost from 1909. Fortunately, girls that age have an extra chamber in the heart, just for storing special secrets. This secret was big, but then so was Cecile's heart.

Cecile would have been content to husk corn for the rest of the morning. She had made an art form of it, an art in which she was a skilled practitioner. But the school year had already begun, and she was missing her studies. Julia sent her inside to read her textbook assignments, while the ladies shucked the rest of the corn.

Oh what a mood Cecile was in! She had never enjoyed such a morning. She had no mind for George Washington and the American Revolution, no enthusiasm for William Shakespeare. Brutus and Mark Antony seemed like a couple of squabbling school kids. Cecile had much grander thoughts, and much deeper feelings. How could she pore through her textbooks? Her heart was about to burst, filled in equal parts by her pride in her ability to contribute and by her growing affection and gratitude for her unlikely new friend and teacher.

She sat on the couch, as she was expected to do, but her choice of books had to match her mood. She took up *The Canterville Ghost* and settled back for an adventure.

"The *Moreauville* Ghost," she said to herself, "Yes, someday I will write about Perry."

She opened the book and began to read aloud, "*When Mr. Hiram B. Otis, the American Minister, bought Canterville Chase, every one told him he was doing a very foolish thing, as there was no doubt at all that the place was haunted."*

Perry appeared as she read, and hearing the end of the line, he asked her, "What place is haunted? This place?" He pointed at her, laughed, and added, "You don't have to tell me."

She wanted to thank him for helping her, not argue again about which of them was dead. The truth is, the more she saw him and the more she thought of him, the more pity she felt. To her, he was no longer just a child who died too young, but a friend, a friend who couldn't face the reality of his own passing.

He asked again, "What place? Are you talking about ghosts?"

She didn't have it in her to speak to him of death and hauntings. His appearance in the living room, which had been a point of fascination, had become a tragic subject. She was grateful for his company, but deeply sorrowful for whatever horror had befallen him in life. She would rather not speak of the horror, so she spoke of her gratitude.

"I did what you told me, and it worked."

He rolled his eyes and answered, "Of course it worked."

Cecile thanked him repeatedly and described the reaction of Julia and Paulina.

Perry was interested in Cecile's family, and he asked their names. She told him about her mother and father, her grandmother, and about her grandfather, cousins, and Great-Aunt Nora. Perry pushed his puckered lips to one side and looked up through the corners of his eyes, trying to dig up memories that weren't there.

He returned his eyes to her and told her, "No, I don't know any of those names. I never heard of a Paulina, but I know Miss Paulie. I work for her daddy. She's such a nice young lady. She's getting married soon. She's not supposed to talk to me. There was one day, I scraped my arm bad, and Miss Paulie wiped up the blood. She held my hand real tender, like she really cared. Her Mamma caught her and yelled at her. She said touching my blood was as bad as marrying me. Wasn't that a funny thing to say? How could we get married? She's a white lady…, must be five years older than me. We don't talk anymore, but she waves at me and smiles, and I know what that means. That means she's my friend."

As he spoke, Cecile's face went stone-still. When he finished, she reanimated, and told him, "Miss Paulie! That must be my Mema. She would have been about that age."

Perry squinted at her and asked, "Are you really from the future, from 1958?"

"I'm not *from* 1958. I'm *in* 1958, and it's not the future. It's right now."

"And I'm *in* 1909. Today is not the past. It's the right now. You're from the future, can't you see?"

Cecile didn't want to speak of morbid topics, and she steered them away from it, "Let's not talk about that. What have you been doing today?"

"I've been picking the crowder peas, but I came in for water. I peeked in to see if you were here, and here you are."

"Here I am. I just sat down to read."

Perry's eyes widened, and he asked excitedly, "You can read? Who taught you how to read?"

"My parents taught me. Can't you read?"

With no shame at all in his voice, he answered, "My Mamma can read some, but not enough to teach me."

The life of a ghost is in the past, and it didn't occur to Cecile that one might have ambitions to learn in death what he never learned in life, so she was surprised when he asked her, "Can you teach me to read? I'm real smart, you'll see."

Without a breath of thought, she blurted, "Yes. I can teach you."

After she said it, she thought about it and wondered what good could come of a dead person learning to read. But she had made the offer and he was very excited. He asked her to read something from the book she held. But it was a ghost story, and ghosts were a sensitive topic.

"No, no, not this one," she said as she stood from the couch and walked to the bookshelf. She rolled her eyes across the line of books and found a worn copy of *Robinson Crusoe*. The binding was loose and many pages within had been folded to mark the spot for some reason or another.

She looked back at Perry. He was not a torso sitting on the floor, but a head and not a whole head. His head from his lower lip up sat in the center of the floor, staring up at her with wide eyes. It was a disturbing image, and Cecile let out a hushed scream.

She gathered her wits and asked, "What has happened to you?"

"Happened?" he asked, "You mean why am I on my knees? Because I didn't know. I didn't know until right now. I can see now that you—"

Still disturbed by the severed head of a boy sitting on the floor in front of her, she interrupted him, demanding, "For Heaven's sake, go back to the way you were."

Without breaking his fixed focus on her, he rose through the floor to be again what he had been, a ghostly boy with no legs.

Cecile was very relieved to see him from the belly up. She released a heavy sigh, drew a deep breath, then asked him, "I'm sorry, what were you saying? You didn't know until now?"

"Yes," he answered with increased reverence, "I'm sorry I called you a ghost. I see now you're an angel. I just thought..., well, I thought angels looked different, you know, like with wings, and maybe a shield or something."

He became suddenly fearful that he might be insulting her appearance, and he rambled on at a quicker, more nervous pace, "You don't need wings. You can fly good without them, and I like your dress. I just thought, well, I'm sorry, I'm glad *you're* my angel."

"Me? An angel? Why do you say that?"

"The way you walked across the air, and you're gunna teach me to read. God heard me! He really heard me, and he sent me an angel."

Cecile walked back to the couch while Perry trembled and stared. She sat down with *Robinson Crusoe*, and she corrected him, "That's a very sweet thing to call me, Perry, but I am *not* an angel. I'm a girl."

He continued to stare with the bright face of a boy who had been visited by God. Clearly, Cecile couldn't convince him that she was just a normal girl, living in the present. She turned the subject to something more practical, "Let's start with this book, *Robinson Crusoe*. I'm supposed to read it at school this year. I might as well start now."

Perry closed his eyes for a moment, trying to imagine what an angel school might look like. The idea of it was beyond him. He abandoned the effort and turned his attention to his Heavenly teacher.

She opened the worn book with dog-eared pages and looked back to him. He was ready to learn, ready to obey. There was an awesome fear in his eyes. That would not do. She wanted her friend back, the one who taught her how to husk corn. She closed the book and begged him, "Perry, will you relax? I am not sent from Heaven. I'm not an angel. I'm just a girl. I guess I *am* from the future, at least from *your* future. But I'm nothing more than a girl. And I'm your friend."

Perry remained silent in thought. He needed more convincing, so she reminded him, "I would think that an angel would know her way around a farm. That's right, an angel wouldn't be crying on a couch because she couldn't husk corn. So you see? I'm just a girl..., and you're just a boy. No more talk of angels or ghosts."

He scratched his head in contemplation. She had made some good points. The most important point was that it didn't matter who was alive, who was dead, from the future, from the past, from Heaven. They were friends. Of that, he had no doubt, so he agreed and cleared his mind for the lesson.

She opened *Robinson Crusoe* again and began, "*I was born in the year 1632, in the city of York...*"

Cecile reviewed the opening line, word-by-word, letter-by-letter, sound-by-sound. He took very quickly to the lesson. When she felt he was ready, she quizzed him.

"B-O-R-N," she challenged him.

"Born!" he blurted quickly.

She nodded her head and continued, "W-A-S,"

This one was harder, but after a few seconds of thought, he declared with pride, "Was!"

"Yes, yes," she encouraged him before continuing, "Y-E-A-R,"

Perry tilted his head and looked out the corner of his eyes, while mouthing something silently. He focused on her again and announced, "That one's easy..., Year!"

Cecile closed the book, held it in one hand, and clapped it with the other. "Hooray! That was wonderful!. Perry, you can read. It's a big book, but you can read the first line, and that's a start."

She had no idea of the effect her congratulations would have on him. His cheeks began to shake, and his eyes filled with tears. He curled his lips into his mouth and bit down on them.

When his soggy eyelids could hold no more, and tears fell down his cheeks, he opened his mouth and repeated three times, "I can read."

"Yes," she said, "There's much more to learn, but you're doing very well. And once you can read, you can do so many things."

"That's true," he said in a high, excited pitch, "*You* said it, so it's true. I can do things. I can be things…, like a doctor. I can be a doctor."

"Yes," Cecile answered, "You can be a great doctor. Perry, you can be a wonderful doctor."

But tears of a different sort rolled down *her* cheeks as she spoke, and when she finished, the rising wave of pity wrinkled her chin and quivered her lips. She knew he would never be a doctor. He would never be anything but what he was — the upper half of a child ghost, for all eternity. And the spirit world has no use for a doctor.

He demanded more, and she gave it. They worked through the next sentence. He struggled with the word "foreigner", but who doesn't? When it seemed he knew all the words, she turned the inside of the book to him. He slid across the floor on his green, ghostly belly, squinted his eyes, and read the whole first paragraph with only a few mistakes.

As he pushed his first unaided syllables from his lips, he looked very real to her. Oh, he was just as ghostly. Green vapors still waved around him. The floorboards and walls could still be seen through him, but that's not what Cecile saw. She saw a boy, a smart, ambitious boy, and she almost began to believe he would succeed, that he just might be a doctor someday.

With the slam of the kitchen door to the outside, Perry disappeared. Paulina came in to prepare dinner. Cecile grabbed one of her textbooks and went into the kitchen. There was a single barstool against the kitchen counter. In the winter or when the workload was light, Cecile's grandfather used to sit there while Paulina cooked. That is the sort of couple they had been. If they were not forced apart by necessary labor, they were by each other's side.

Paulina was glad to have Cecile on that stool. It was hard for her not to talk, but Cecile had studying to do, so Paulina sang quietly. It was a way for them to converse without interrupting the reading assignment. After three different songs, and one of them sung twice, Paulina couldn't help herself.

She spoke softly, "*Ti cher*, no work this afternoon. We've got to do the visits."

The chapter Cecile was reading in her history book was interesting. Well, the topic was, but it was poorly written to hold the attention of a child with a heart like Cecile's. The wording was dry and utterly devoid of feeling. Cecile was sure she could write it better. So she welcomed Paulina's interruption, closing the book with vigor and setting it on the counter like she intended never to open it again.

"Visits?" she asked with piqued curiosity.

"Oh, yes," Paulina spoke with her signature melodic tones, "Ya'll have been here a whole day now. We have to make the visits. It would be insulting not to."

"Who are we visiting?"

Paulina began a long list of required homes to see. Not all of the homes were above ground. Yes, the dead must also be visited. Cecile knew which visits were to houses and which were to graves. The title "Poor" always preceded the names of the dead.

"We have to see Alice and Poor Oscar. Then we have to visit your cousin Ti Jean. He thinks he's preparing for college, but all he's doing is running down his poor daddy's farm."

While Paulina spoke, Cecile mouthed to herself, "Okay, Ti Jean and Alice are living. Oscar and Ti Jean's daddy are dead."

By the time the list was finished, there were as many dead as living. The visits to the dead were just as important, this was clear. And Paulina spoke of them as if the visits would be greatly appreciated. Cecile would not have known she spoke of graves, except for the word "Poor" before the names.

The list was not some dry textbook, like the one Cecile had put down. Oh no, it was not just a tally of names. Each name came with a story, either funny or tragic, and some lofty praise or harsh judgment, but even judgment was delivered with love in her voice.

After dinner, they left the house, not in Paulina's car, though it seemed perfectly fit for the occasion. Paulina hitched the horse to the wagon and drove it to the front door. The car *would* have done fine, but the visits were steeped in tradition, so they were performed traditionally. The car would also have been much faster. The distance between farms was extensive. They went south, almost to Plaucheville, and as far north as Bordelonville, and saw half a dozen homes and twice as many graves.

The visits with the Cajun relatives were, well, very Cajun. An excessive amount of food was served, and talk was free and open. Cajuns don't shy away from any topics, even death. It was one of the common themes that sewed all the visits together. Cousin Alice, still in her prime, brought Cecile to her closet, where she showed off her funeral dress. There it would hang for the many decades until her death.

Alice was the first visit, and Cecile felt awkward and uncomfortable as she complimented Alice's funeral dress. City-talk is very different. Cecile didn't know how to respond to, "Won't I look pretty in it?" But after a few visits, a few talkative meals, the Cajun view of death seemed quite normal. Watching Paulina talk in casual conversation to the graves they visited, as if those beneath the dirt were pleased to be kept in the loop, quickly went from unsettling to endearing. Cecile's blood was half-Cajun, but it is safe to say she became truly Cajun that day.

There was one common thread sewn through all the visits, both house and grave alike. It was the Great Flood of 1927. The event left a deep bruise in the culture of the community. Many of the dates marked on the graves ended with 1927. Avoyelles Parish was devastated. Farms were destroyed and many people didn't escaped the waters. And the Cajuns, being Cajun, spoke of it openly and in morbid detail.

They described where and how one cousin or another was found dead. 1927 claimed much of the family, and the aunts, uncles, and cousins who survived it still cried when they spoke of it. They still talked of life and love, of hope in the future, but it all blended with death in that signature Cajun way. By the time they made their last stop, late in the day, Cecile felt like she understood them in a way she never had before.

Just south of Bordelonville was a quaint little farmhouse. From the outside, in the deep dusk, it looked worn down, more from neglect than from time.

Cecile thought, "This must be Ti Jean's house."

The thought was followed immediately by the opening door. A disheveled man stood in the doorway, friendly as a puppy, but messy. All of the other people they had visited were dressed special for the occasion — not this young man. His shirt was half-untucked and his fly was open.

Paulina belted out, "Cawww, Ti Jean, look at you. Straighten yourself up for your cousins."

Ti Jean made a half attempt to pat down his hair. He gave no effort to his shirt or fly. But when they walked into the house, oooh, what a succulent aroma. Ti Jean could cook! He had prepared a sausage gumbo.

"Three different kinds of sausage!" he boasted.

During the meal, each time he spoke of the gumbo, the number of different sausages went up by one. By the time they finished eating, Ti Jean was bragging about his seven-sausage gumbo.

It was late in the evening, and they stayed the night at Ti Jean's. This distressed Cecile. She had rather hoped to sleep at her Mema's, on the couch in the living room, and just maybe see Perry. The late hours were spent with whiskey and soda, and plenty of stories. Of course, there was talk about the dead, and there were ghost stories, which only made Cecile miss Perry more. The Cajuns spoke of ghosts not in terms of terror, but almost as if they wished to be haunted. It made Cecile feel like her friendship with Perry was something quite normal, quite Cajun.

They moved from the dining room to the living room to play at cards. Cecile was too exhausted from the surging waves of emotion and in no mood to play games with others. She crawled into the bed she would share with her mother and Mema. That night she slept little. She pictured Perry's excited face and thought about the wasted potential. In the hours before Julia and Paulina joined her, she cried. Through her tears, she whispered to herself, "Someday he will come to know that he's dead and will never be more than he is."

Chapter Five:
Silly Ghost Talk

OF ALL THE WONDERS OF THEIR DAY OF VISITING, one thing struck Cecile most deeply. Her extended family spoke of and spoke to the dead as if they were ever-present. It gave Cecile the courage to talk about Perry without being judged. By the time they rolled away from Ti Jean's messy house in the early morning, nothing of the sort still seemed strange.

Nature herself was slow to rise that morning. There was a peaceful quiet to the air. The roll of the wagon wheels was the only sound they could hear as they made their way back to Moreauville. There was an unusual absence of conversation, and Cecile got sucked into that void.

While Julia dozed in and out of a shallow sleep in the back of the wagon, Cecile joined Paulina on the coach box. After less than a minute by her side, she asked, "Mema, have you ever seen a ghost?"

After all the visits to the graves, conversations with and about the dead, and ghost stories to boot, the question didn't surprise Paulina. In fact, she expected it. She answered with a smile, "Not like in the books, no white sheets or rattling chains. But I've seen things. I've heard things and felt things that I believe were my poor loved ones reaching out to me."

41

Cecile scooted closer and asked, "Were you scared?"

"Of my parents? Of your grandfather? Never! It's always a strange feeling, no doubt of that, but love is eternal. A parent in life is a parent in death." Paulina dropped her head in thought of her husband, and added, "A lover in life is a lover in death."

Paulina was still a widow in mourning. Her shoulders began to shake, as she said through her cry, *"Ti cher*, your grandfather loved you so much, and he loves you still."

Cecile leaned hard into her Mema and threw one arm tightly around her back. They rolled on without talk for the next several minutes, while Paulina's cry swelled and diminished, from a few sniffles to full sobs and back again.

After she settled down, she asked Cecile, "How about you? Have you ever seen a ghost?"

Paulina expected a quick and clear "No." What she got instead spoke volumes. Cecile withdrew her arm from Paulina's back, held her hands together between her tightly pressed knees, and slouched as if she was trying to withdraw into her dress like a turtle into the shell. She had wanted to talk about Perry. She began the conversation with that very intention, but now that it came to it, she was afraid. Whether she was afraid for her or afraid for Perry, she herself couldn't have said.

There was no mistaking the reaction. Cecile had seen something, something she hesitated to talk about. Paulina saw that clearly, and she reminded her grandchild, "Cher, you know you can tell your Mema anything."

She put her arm over Cecile's shoulders, gave her a squeeze, then retook the reins. Cecile didn't fear her Mema's judgment. That wasn't the reason for the silence. Perry was more than a supernatural occurrence. There was something deeper she couldn't yet speak of, because she didn't understand it herself.

Cecile was a warm and kind girl. She made friends quickly and loved them dearly, but never like this. Aside from the obvious, Perry was different. She had only just met him, yet he was *in her* like no other friend. She may have only seen him in the living room of her Mema's farmhouse, but he haunted her heart constantly. Her thoughts of him were intense and emotional, simultaneously bright and dark, hopeful and tragic, promising and pitiful. It felt to Cecile like she had always known him, like they had been friends since birth. She couldn't have possibly put it into words, so she remained thoughtfully silent, comforted by the feeling that her Mema understood her, even if she didn't know the details.

After about ten minutes of deep thoughtfulness, like a hermit within her own dress, Cecile enlivened. She looked to Paulina and asked, "Do you think…, maybe sometimes…, a person, a dead person, doesn't know he's dead? Like maybe, if you see a ghost and he thinks he's still alive?"

Paulina returned the same arm to Cecile's shoulders and answered, "How could that be? I imagine being dead is very different than being alive. All I feel from the dead is love. I guess when nothing else still matters, love is all that's left. It doesn't sound so bad, does it?"

"But what if there were things they wanted to do but they never got the chance? Like, what if they die young and never learn to read. Do you think they would still want to?"

Paulina took a moment to think about it, then she answered honestly, "Mon sucre, I don't know."

It was clear Cecile's questions were not purely academic. She was deeply affected by something. No loving Cajun Mema could have missed that. Yet Paulina was hesitant to pry for fear of returning Cecile to her shell.

After a few minutes without words, Paulina tried to gently respark the conversation, "*Whatever* they're going through, the dead, if they come to us, they come to us for a good reason. It's best we open our hearts to them."

Cecile didn't respond, but she smiled wide upon hearing this. It made her feel good to think Perry had come to her for a reason, that destiny had forced the encounter. Paulina wanted badly to ask her what she had experienced that brought on such questions, but it was enough for her to look at Cecile and see the widening smile.

After a few more minutes of quiet, Cecile finally asked, "Have you ever heard of any ghosts in your house?"

Paulina answered without a breath of pause, "Cher, you're asking if my house is haunted? Of course it is. How could it be otherwise? It has always been a house of love, and who would ever want to leave that?"

That same wide smile burst back onto Cecile's face, and she said, "If it's okay, when we get back, I might try to talk to them, to the ghosts, I mean."

"Well," Paulina responded, with a few pats of Cecile's back, "I'm sure they will be happy for your attention."

Suddenly, a motherly voice rang out from behind them, "Enough of the silly ghost talk. Mamma, why are you encouraging this?"

Paulina patted Cecile a few more times, then, without turning around, shouted back to her daughter, "How long have you been listening?"

"Long enough to worry about you two."

In the same voice she used to soothe Julia when she was a child, she said, "Aww cher, it's all innocence."

Julia, with a little more sternness in her voice, demanded, "Well, enough of it for now. Talk about other things. When we get back home, Cecile's trying out for the school talent show. Isn't that right, Sweetie? Your Mema wants to hear all about that. No more talk of ghosts."

Cecile obeyed and told Paulina about the song and dance she had been practicing. She told her about the last year's show, of who had talent and who did not. The things coming from Cecile's mouth satisfied Julia. But her mind and her mouth worked together without her heart. Her heart was elsewhere. Her heart was with Perry.

There was no more ghost talk for the rest of the ride back to Moreauville. None of them had gotten much sleep, so when they got back, they all needed to rest. Cecile slept in her mother's bed, but not before a slow and watchful walk through the living room.

Once she was asleep, Julia confronted Paulina, "Cecile worries me sometimes, the things she talks about, asking about farmhands dying on the farm, being cut in half. All the silly ghost talk might seem innocent enough, but I don't think it's good for her."

Paulina would never step on her daughter's maternal rights, but she was the matriarch of the family, and that entitled her to an opinion and the right to express it.

She kissed Julia and acknowledged, "You're right, cher, she says some strange things. I'll give you that. But that's because she's a strange child."

Julia tilted her head at Paulina and scolded her with her eyebrows.

Paulina corrected herself, "I mean…she's *special*, special in ways I don't think we understand. She has thoughts beyond her years. And I think it's best we let her get them out, however she can."

Julia admitted, "She *has* seemed much more thoughtful lately."

Paulina nodded, kissed her daughter again, and added, "Oh, I'm sure she'll continue to surprise us…, surprise and delight us."

Julia took a step back, stared at her mother thoughtfully, then responded, "Well, I'm sure you're right. Cecile will say what she wants to say. She always has. Still, I don't think we should talk so much about the dead. It's such a sad thing for her to dwell on."

Paulina had a way of getting in the last word. She walked Julia to the guest bedroom, kissed her, and turned toward her own room. Just two steps away, she commented under her breath, "Caww, you've been in the city too long."

It was such a Paulina thing to do, Julia could only smile. Paulina's opinions were sticky. They had a way of clinging to people. Still standing at the threshold of the guest room, with her sweetly sleeping daughter nearby, and her mother now shut up in her own room, Julia whispered to herself, "Mamma's probably right. With all those graves she saw, and all those stories, I guess it's only natural."

Julia slept easy, much more so than if she had known the truth — that her only child had spoken openly with a glowing green apparition, that she was growing to care for this phantom child, and that the connection between them had already rooted itself deeply into Cecile's heart.

Chapter Six:
Untouchable Goodness

MOST OF WHAT THE FARM PRODUCED was meant for market, but they kept a patch of sugar cane for family use. They also kept a chicken coop for their own eggs. Any excess in sugar or eggs was traded with the neighboring farms for ham, bacon, fresh milk, or any staple not produced on their own farm. Bartering was a way for the community to be self-sufficient. There was little consumed in Avoyelles Parish that was not produced in Avoyelles Parish.

It would have been ideal to harvest the sugar cane a month later, when the sugar was at its peak. The circumstances didn't allow it. The morning after they returned from the visits, Julia and Paulina went to the sugar cane patch. Cecile joined them, expecting to be useful. Paulina had another form of usefulness in mind for her granddaughter.

The conversation in the cart made one thing clear to Paulina. Cecile was seeing something in the farmhouse, something she was reluctant to tell. Paulina, missing her late husband terribly, hoped that *he* might be the ghost Cecile was seeing. Julia and Paulina chopped the cane, and Cecile carried it to the barn. That arrangement lasted only an hour. Paulina wanted Cecile in the house, where she might commune with the departed.

After an hour of carrying cane stalks, Cecile's arms and legs were sore, and she needed to rest. Paulina gave her a short stick of sugar cane for her to chew on, and sent her inside. Julia was too busy cutting to notice, so she said nothing when their little beast-of-burden skipped inside with a stick of sugar cane at her mouth like a flute.

Cecile sat on the couch chewing on sugar cane and sipping water for about twenty minutes, while her fixed eyes never left the wood floor in the center of the living room. And suddenly, she was not alone. It was not Cecile's grandfather in the green haze that formed in the living room. It was Perry.

Cecile began telling Perry about her visits to the relatives, but he stopped her short, saying, "I don't have time to talk. I need to be working. But I'm happy to see you. I snuck in here four more times yesterday, but you didn't come."

Cecile tried to imagine what sort of work he could be doing. What kind of labor could a ghost undertake?

She asked him, and he answered, "I picked the crowder peas yesterday, and now I need to shell them."

The crowder peas! That's what Paulina and Julia had planned for the next day.

"Oooh, you have to show me how!" she demanded, "They'll be surprised, just like the corn. Perry, show me. Show me how to shell the crowder peas."

Perry looked around to see if anyone was watching him. When he saw the chance, he slid a few feet toward the kitchen and disappeared. Cecile didn't wait long. He appeared within a minute with a fist full of pea pods.

"You see this vein?" he asked her, "You gotta start there. Pull along the vein with these fingers, and open the shell with these. And the peas fall right in your hand."

What he did next seemed magical. He appeared to wave his hand over the pod before it split open and the peas rolled out.

"Again, again," she demanded enthusiastically, "but slower this time."

He turned to give her a better angle, then slowly pinched the vein and pulled it along the pod. In the same motion, with his middle two fingertips, he pried the pod open, and out came the peas. Cecile was too excited to thank him. She ran to the pea field and picked a few to try. When she got back to the living room, Perry was gone.

She attempted his technique on the first pod, tearing the pod in half and crushing the peas. She tried on the second, more slowly this time. The peas rolled onto her palm like actors in a play, stepping out for their bows.

"Thank you, Perry," she shouted, "If you can hear me."

This new skill could not wait for the next day. She hurried out to the pea field with a basket, and she filled it with freshly picked pea pods. She returned to the living room, just in case Perry might reappear. Sitting on the couch, with the basket of pea pods on the floor in front of her, one on the couch to her left for the empty shells, and a basin beside her for the shelled peas, she began to work. She was slow at first, meticulously imitating Perry, but she sped up with each pod. By the time she was halfway through the basket, she was as quick as Perry. Before she knew it, the basket was empty, and she ran outside to refill it.

It took three baskets of whole pods to fill the basin with peas, but she filled the basin before Paulina or Julia came back inside. The work was not laborious, but delightful, and she couldn't wait to see the look on her Mema's face. She decided to stage the basin of peas dramatically on the table, a glorious centerpiece to catch their eyes when they came in for dinner. But when she went into the kitchen there was already someone there. Aunt Nora had come by and let herself in through the kitchen door. She came to make dinner for them.

It was sugar cane day, and Nora knew this, so she was surprised to see Cecile come in from the living room with a basin of freshly shelled peas.

Nora turned and praised her, "Caww, look there! Did you shell all those by yourself?"

Cecile beamed with pride as she answered, "I sure did!"

"You must have learned that from your Mamma. She was always the best at shelling peas."

Cecile was too proud to think clearly, and she answered without realizing what she was saying, "No, Perry taught me. I'm going to surprise Mema and Mamma when they come in for dinner."

Cecile staged her centerpiece with no thought to what she had just said. Nora stared at her in disbelief. She only knew of one Perry in all her years in the parish.

While Cecile adjusted the basin, Nora asked her with wide eyes of disbelief, "Perry taught you? Have you seen Perry?"

Cecile went as still as a statue, and the blood rushed from her face. She was a quick-witted girl, and a little deceitful when she needed to be. She answered with her very next breath, "Not Perry. I don't know any Perry. I said Mary."

"Well who's Mary?"

"Mary? She's my friend at school. She taught me."

Nora shook it off as a misunderstanding and thought no more of Perry. Her response made one thing clear to Cecile — There *was* a boy named Perry, and Great-Aunt Nora knew of him. That nagging little part of Cecile's brain that told her Perry was just in her imagination was put to rest. Perry was real, or at least he had been.

Paulina and Julia walked in at the end of the exchange, having heard nothing to raise an eyebrow. Cecile had a friend at school named Mary who taught her something. There was nothing abnormal in what they heard. What they *saw* astonished them, a large basin filled with shelled crowder peas.

Paulina nodded to her sister in appreciation, then winked at Cecile and said, "Looks like you and Aunt Nora have been working hard."

Nora raised her hands and contradicted her, "Don't look at me. I just got here. Cecile did that by herself."

Julia asked Nora, "When did you teach her how to shell peas?"

Nora shook her head and answered, "I was just as surprised as you."

Paulina had attributed the husked corn to some latent farmer blood in her veins, but the peas? This was extraordinary, and Paulina's hopes were bolstered. She had no doubt that her husband had come to Cecile, spoken with her and taught her. She was desperate to talk to her granddaughter about it, to reconnect with her late husband through the precious teenage medium who sat with her bright blush and proud smile in front of her basin of peas.

This was not the time for such a sensitive discussion. Nora suggested that the ladies teach Cecile how to make the family's andouille and boudin jambalaya. The family roots that had withered and nearly died in Cecile before her grandfather's death were thriving and taking hold of her innermost being. The idea of learning a secret family recipe made those roots pulse in rhythm with her heartbeat. She jumped up from her chair and hopped onto the kitchen counter beside the stove, crossing her legs at the ankles and kicking the cabinets with her heels in excitement.

Well, that was that. Peas and corn didn't matter, nor ghosts or young mediums. It was ladies' day in the kitchen, and the four of them bonded over rice and sausages, onions, celery, and peppers, and most importantly, over a secret blend of spices that had passed from mother to daughter in that very kitchen since the year the home was built.

They cooked together, told stories, laughed until they cried, and cried until they laughed again. The efforts ended with the most loving meal the old table had ever hosted, filled with that magical sort of feminine affection that can only be felt in such company.

After dinner, there was no question what Cecile would be doing with her afternoon. An entire field of crowder peas awaited her inexplicable talent. Nora cleaned and returned home. Paulina and Julia returned to the sugar cane, and Cecile, ahead of schedule, began the harvesting of crowder peas. She had already proven to be infinitely more useful than expected. Even Adam, had he been able to stay, would not have contributed so much. So nobody cared that she went inside an hour before supper.

She didn't fling herself on the couch because she was exhausted. In fact, she pulsed with energy. She grabbed *Robinson Crusoe* and waited for Perry. She read ahead to pass the time, but before long, the vapors formed and Perry appeared among them.

"Did you shell the peas like I showed you?" he asked her.

"Oh yes, I did great, as good as you."

She was struck by his expression and his deep gaze into her face. He had been a friendly young ghost that she was growing to appreciate and deeply pity, but in that look she saw something more. It was not a look of curious fascination at a ghostly apparition, or the reverent gaze at a Heavenly angel. It was a look of esteem with a strong strand of adoration.

He opened his big, brown eyes even wider, and said, "I know you did great. You're…, you're…,"

Her heart begged for the next word, but it didn't come. He simply stared at her with his wide eyes and gaping mouth.

She prompted him, "I'm what?"

He shook himself from the emotions that froze him, emotions he didn't really understand, recovered his normal expression, and said, "You're reading some more."

"Yes, listen and try to imagine the letters."

She read the first few paragraphs of the book, but after she read, "*My father, a wise and grave man, gave me serious and excellent counsel…*"

He interrupted, "*My* father is a grave man."

She lowered the book, eager to learn about his family, and asked him, "Really? Who is your father?"

"Not who *is* he."

"Who *was* he?" she corrected herself quickly, "Did your father die?"

He looked confused and a little frustrated. Not sure if she was teasing him, he answered, "I just said that. He's a *grave* man."

Cecile suddenly realized the point of confusion, and she corrected him, "No, that's not what that means, not a person in a grave. It means a serious person."

He understood his mistake, but had not yet recovered. He still looked at her sternly, so she asked, "How did he die?"

Perry took a deep breath, held it for a few seconds, let it out and answered, "They killed him. I was just a baby. I don't remember him."

Cecile, deeply concerned, pried, "Who killed him? Why did they kill him?"

Perry seemed more relaxed as he answered, "It wasn't here, not these people. Oh no, they're real nice. Mamma says they love us, and it feels like they do, especially Miss Paulie. We even get our own dishes. We don't eat off their dishes, so they have special dishes for us."

What felt like an honor to Perry mortified Cecile. She knew why they got their own dishes. Whites would not use the same dishes used by blacks.

She brushed that aside and returned to her real curiosity, "Who killed your father? How did he die?"

"We used to live north, by Shreveport. Mamma says he tried to get a job, a special job, a good job, and that made them mad. They hanged him from a tree, so we came down here. Now we work on the farms here, and they're very nice to us."

Perry didn't speak with anger. There was no hatred in his tone. Cecile felt like someone had punched her in the chest. The physical manifestations of her deep, compassionate pity were real. She began to cough as her face reddened and her eyebrows furled above her watery eyes.

Perry didn't immediately connect her suddenly changed condition with what he had just told her. With concern, he asked, "Cecile, what's wrong? Are you gunna be all right?"

Cecile recovered instantly. Such an amazing boy she saw in front of her! His life had been tragic from his earliest days, his childhood laborious, and his death, well, Cecile still couldn't bring herself to think about it. Yet here he was, with no self-pity, no anger, and not a thought of retribution. His eyes were fixed on his friend, with selfless concern for her well-being.

Cecile had never felt such a desire to throw her arms around someone. Her mind was occupied with a hundred thoughts in swirling chaos, so her body obeyed the dictates of her heart. She flew from her seat on the couch. Before she realized she was in motion, she was kneeling on the floor, face-to-face with Perry.

Her movement was so sudden and forceful, it startled Perry. He leaned back, but when she stopped in front of him, and he saw the loving look on her face, he leaned forward again, until they were mere inches apart. Had she focused her eyes on the wall behind him, she would have easily seen through him. But to her, at that moment, he wasn't a ghost. There was nothing phantom-like about him. He was a boy filled with goodness, a rare, quality human being, and a treasured friend. No, no, she didn't see the wall behind him. She looked into his eyes, and her vision stopped there.

She put her arms around him, but of course, she couldn't touch him. Her arms passed right through him without the slightest sensation of contact. She slowly wrapped her arms around herself, dropped her head into her tightly folded arms, and began to cry softly.

She closed her eyes and cried until she heard him say, "Aww, Cecile, you see, I knew you were an angel."

She opened her eyes, raised them to him, took a deep sniff, then asked, "What?"

"You must be an angel," he explained with a content grin, "You have *God's* love. *People* don't love like that."

She sat back on her heels and dropped her arms to her side. She looked at him, then through him. She took notice of the wall behind him, studied the green vapors that surrounded him, and for the first time she thought, maybe he isn't the ghost of some farmhand who died on the farm. Maybe he is something else. He had appeared to her when she was sad and taught her how to end her sadness. He seemed to say what she needed to hear, when she needed to hear it. He was filled with pure, compassionate goodness. Maybe it's *Perry* who is the angel.

Chapter Seven:
Hers and Hers Alone

AFTER THE FAILED EMBRACE, Cecile was determined to spend more time with Perry, drawn in equal parts by academic curiosity and by a deep, mystic, and rapidly swelling affection. For the next couple of days, she divided her time between chores on the farm and in the house, her neglected studies, and the appearances of Perry in the living room. When he came to her, they traded in skills. He taught her the best way to fetch the eggs from the hen house without being attacked by the hens. She read to him and taught him to read, chipping their way together through *Robinson Crusoe*.

Sunday came, a day of rest, and aside from the morning trip to St. Peter Church in Bordelonville, the day was to be spent in calm conversation. There was one problem with this. The living room would not be Cecile's alone, and she was beginning to understand that Perry wouldn't come to her anywhere else. In the afternoon, she sat on the corner of the couch where she always sat. Paulina sat on the other end, and Julia was in the chair on the adjacent wall. Julia knitted while humming softly. Paulina read. Cecile simply sat and stared at the floor.

She wasn't looking for Perry or waiting for him to appear. One constant about his appearances was that he came to her when nobody else was around and disappeared when anybody else came.

Cecile wasn't sleepy, but her mind drifted in shallow daydreams. Her mother's soft humming was a lullaby that soothed her consciousness to sleep and left her subconscious with full reign of her thoughts. She thought of Perry, with her half-focused eyes gazing at the spot where he always appeared. She replayed their conversations in her head, and imagined some new ones, all while Julia hummed in the background.

Cecile pictured Perry's green vapors appearing as they always did. She saw in her mind his figure taking form, poking out of the wood floor from the waist up. She saw his mouth open and heard him start to sing. It suddenly struck her, as her consciousness surged back onto the scene and retook control of her mind — she wasn't *imagining* Perry, but seeing him and hearing him.

In a panic, she looked to her mother, who still hummed in a locked focus on her knitting. She turned to Paulina, who casually turned the page of her book. Perry looked right at her, clearly not noticing the others. He sang for her, but she couldn't appreciate it. She couldn't listen. She gestured to her Mema at the end of the couch and held her finger to her lips.

He continued to sing, so she whispered, "Ssshhhh."

Paulina looked up from her book. If Perry had been at all visible to her, she would surely have seen him as she turned her attention to Cecile. She didn't notice him, and only said to Cecile, "Aww, let your Mamma sing. She sounds so sweet."

Julia looked at Cecile on the couch, then drifted her eyes to Paulina, and said, "Thanks, Mamma."

Julia had looked right through Perry and said nothing of him. She saw nothing of him, and heard nothing of him. She returned to her knitting as Perry sang more loudly.

It was obvious to Cecile that Perry was hers and hers alone. Nobody else could see or hear him. Nobody questioned the strange green vapors waving above the floor. They just returned to their calm and quiet activities. Cecile passed her eyes back and forth several times, from Perry to Julia, to Perry again and to Paulina. Not only did her mother and grandmother say nothing about Perry, Perry said nothing about them.

With her whole hand, Cecile grabbed her jaw beneath her nose and thought, finally thinking to herself, "They can't see each other. He comes to me and me alone."

With that realization, she sat back and listened to Perry. He sang, getting louder and louder as the song swelled his feelings. It was an old spiritual hymn, sacred yet bluesy. It spoke of hardship and of hope. Above all, it was a song of gratitude to God for all blessings. Perry's voice was high and pure, and it echoed like an organ in an empty church.

On and on Perry sang about the great Blessings of the Lord. When he brought the song to a slowly diminishing and sweet conclusion, he looked at her with his wide, brown eyes, and told her, "We were singing that song in church this morning. It made me think of you, and I said a prayer. I said a prayer for you and thanked God for sending you to me. They have books in the church, you know, with the songs and things from the Bible. I picked one up, and you know what? I read some of it. I read it and understood it. Of course it made me think about you, and ohhh, I was so grateful. The song meant so much more and I decided. I decided I would come here, even though it's Sunday, and I would sing the song for you. Miss Paulie let me in, *on a Sunday*! I knew she would. They were all in the kitchen. I came in here and here you are."

Her heart felt as if it had expanded beyond her rib cage. She lost all notice of her mother and grandmother, and replied to him, "I *am* here, and so are you!"

Paulina, not pulling her nose from her book, responded, "Yea cher, we're all here."

Cecile raised her shoulders, covered her mouth, and giggled. She wanted to ask Perry if he could see anyone else on the couch with her, but how could she without drawing the attention of Julia and Paulina?

For the briefest moment she thought that maybe she was crazy. Maybe Perry was a hallucination in the failing mind of a sick child, but quickly she silently argued with herself, "Perry couldn't come from my mind. He has taught me things I didn't know. He's wonderful in ways I could not have imagined."

She defeated her own doubts in that short, internal debate, and focused her full attention again on Perry. He stared at her with a smile that would have hurt a face less used to smiling.

He asked her, "What do you think? Did you like the song? I can't stay. Tell me, Cecile, did you like the song?"

He had paid her a wonderful compliment, which required an answer. She had no idea how to reply with Julia and Paulina sitting in quiet ignorance nearby. Yet, she couldn't ignore him. He had placed himself in a vulnerable position, confessing feelings to her that could not be left unanswered. She did the only thing she could think to do. She stood from the couch, kissed her fingertips, took the step to stand in front of him, touched her kissed fingers to the air where his cheek appeared, smiled widely at him, winked, and walked out of the room.

She walked into the kitchen, fixed herself a glass of sweet tea, and sat on the stool by the counter. She dwelled intensely on the song and his explanation of it. Verse by verse, she tried to recall the words. The full weight of his meaning settled on her. Warmth radiated from the depths of her soul, and she felt herself blush across her entire body. Never had she had such a friend, someone who admired and appreciated her so much. She had never had friends who sang songs of gratitude to God for putting her in their lives.

These intense realizations coupled with the revelation that Perry was hers and hers alone. She didn't know *what* he was. She thought, "A ghost would surely have been seen by others, or maybe not."

If he was an angel, he was unlike any described by priest, nun, or scripture. As she sat on the stool enveloped in the warmth of his affection and gratitude, even the thought that he was a figment of her imagination didn't bother her. All she knew was that the living room floor in her Mema's house was a very special place, a sacred and holy place. It was Cecile and Perry's own personal playground.

As she considered this, her warmth faded and her heart sank. She had two more weeks until harvest was done and she must go back to New Orleans. The idea of not seeing Perry until the spring of the next year broke her heart. She felt the sudden need to see him again, and she walked back into the living room with her tea. Julia still knitted and hummed. Paulina still read. The floor was just a floor.

She walked through the living room and straight to the guest bedroom. She laid down and hoped with all of her hope that her silent gesture had its intended effect, that Perry felt her full affection in the touch of her kissed fingers — a touch she knew he couldn't feel.

She laid for a full hour in emotional agitation. When she finally walked back into the living room, Julia had gone into the kitchen to make sandwiches. Paulina sat reading as she had been. Cecile felt a strong desire to speak of Perry, but had no idea how to begin. She sat beside her Mema and thought about the farm, about her grandfather and cousins, and all who had passed through that very living room over the generations. She remembered Poor Celeste and interrupted Paulina's reading.

"Mema," she asked, "Can you tell me about Poor Celeste?"

"Poor Celeste? Aww, Poor Celeste was the dearest woman. She worked for us for a long time. To tell you the truth, cher, I loved her very much. I could have never told my daddy that. But we all loved her. She was different from the other servants. She was like family."

It was the perfect distraction from thoughts of Perry. Cecile's curiosity was piqued, and she asked, "Why couldn't you tell your daddy?"

"Poor Celeste was a colored woman, an unmarried colored woman with a child. I don't know why she kept working for us. Her son grew up and got a *good* job. She had money. She didn't need us. But she kept coming. We couldn't pay her much, but she kept working here, until she got sick. I think she loved us. She thanked us every day for all we did for her, though it's hard to imagine what we did. We didn't make her any richer, that's for sure."

"When did she die?"

"Oh, I guess almost fifteen years now. We sure miss her still. She was all the time so sweet to us, and so grateful. And cawww, she worked so hard."

"She didn't need the money, and you don't know why she stayed?"

"I told you, cher, this is a house of love, and nobody wants to leave it."

It seemed the perfect explanation, and Cecile gave it little more thought. But she couldn't help but consider, maybe Perry had appeared to Poor Celeste too, and Poor Celeste was as reluctant to leave him as Cecile was.

Whomever Perry had belonged to in the past. He belonged to Cecile in 1958, and she went to bed that night praying that he would still be hers in the spring, listing in her prayers all of the reasons she still needed him, and begging God not to take him away from her.

Chapter Eight:
I Will Carry You Thither in Charity

KNOWING PERRY COULD BE SEEN BY NOBODY but Cecile liberated their relationship in many ways. Within a couple days, Perry told her that she could not be seen or heard by "his people." This came as a great relief to Cecile, who wondered since she met Perry how many spirits roamed the old farmhouse. She placed herself more often in the living room, taking up chores that could be done on a couch.

Perry, too, promised to make a greater effort to see her. Cecile struggled to imagine what sort of impediments might keep a ghost (or an angel) from appearing where and when he wishes, why he couldn't come to her every time and every moment she made her way to the living room couch. Whatever was the cause, he was true to his word, and he appeared more regularly in his spot on the floor.

The more time they spent together, the more they laughed and learned, and the faster the days flew by. Cecile tried to encourage Perry's ambitions by teaching him to read an old book on Cajun home remedies. The medical credibility of the book would be almost entirely debunked by any medical professional, but that didn't matter to the children. Perry's ambitions soared along with Cecile's silent pity in equal proportion.

Perry's reading came along quickly, as did Cecile's proficiency on the farm. But Cecile wasn't in Moreauville to be a literacy teacher. She was there to help Paulina with the harvest, and much too early for her or Perry, the harvest was done. The three weeks were over, and a life she knew well but thought little of awaited her in New Orleans.

On the last full day, Adam joined them. Cousins and uncles came to Paulina's farm with their trucks and helped to load the harvest for transport.

Cecile asked her Mema, "Where's it all going?"

Paulina, wanting to boost Cecile's pride in her work, told her, "Well, cher, we'll take the corn you husked and the peas you shelled to the Bayou Des Glaises. They'll load it onto boats and take it to Simmesport for sale. From there, that same corn and peas will go on big boats on the Atchafalaya River, then to the Mississippi and then to dinner tables all over the country. You see, boo, it's very important, what we do here."

For Cecile, there was no thinking about husked corn or shelled peas without thinking of the boy who taught her how. Paulina's words made Perry seem all the more wonderful. She thought about Perry's reading and of his pride and ambitions. Perhaps nothing could ever come of his learning to read, but it made him happy. After a life of hardship, at least in the spirit world, he could be happy, and she was the one who taught him how.

She pondered this while staring directly at Paulina, then she answered, "Yes, Mema, I see. What we do here is very important."

Cecile, with her scant frame, could be of no use loading crops onto boats. She couldn't help bargain prices in Simmesport. In short, there was no more she could contribute to the harvest, at least not for sale. Between the house and the barn was a miniature farm in itself, a small plot of land no larger than the house. It was there they grew the produce for their own consumption. When the farm emptied of everyone but her, Cecile went there to gather food for the pantry and to snack on food fresh off the vines.

The pride of this garden was the creole tomatoes. To a shopper choosing produce in a store, they would have looked repulsive. They were oddly shaped tomatoes, lumpy, with what looked to Cecile like scars across their faces. Oh, but they were scrumptious, sweet and rich in earthy flavor. The creole tomatoes, like everything else grown in Avoyelles Parish, came from the Mississippi Delta soil, the richest farmland in the country.

Cecile sat among the plants and picked and ate a tomato. She tried to imagine the farm in 1909, to picture Perry working under the same sun that beat down on her. She couldn't touch him. She couldn't give him a hug or hold his hand. But she placed her hand on the dirt beside her and thought maybe, just maybe, Perry had walked across that very spot. She couldn't feel Perry, but she could feel the ground where he once walked, and at that moment, it was good enough for her.

It suddenly dawned on her. Perry often spoke of working the farm. She stood and looked around, thinking that just maybe she could catch a glimpse of him haunting the fields in fruitless labor. She didn't see him, but she felt him. That is to say, she thought and felt so intensely of him that it seemed like he was right there beside her, among the creole tomatoes.

She picked another tomato, took one bite, and carried it inside. With a partially eaten tomato in her hand, she sat on the couch and waited. Perry appeared with a creole tomato in *his* hand, and Cecile's heart skipped a beat.

She exclaimed, "You were there, right where I sat. I knew you were there. I just knew it!"

He smiled at her excitement but had no idea what she was talking about, and he asked her.

She answered, "I was just in the garden with the tomatoes. I was thinking about you, and I just knew you were there."

"I *was* in the garden," he confirmed, "Miss Paulie told me I could get a tomato. But I didn't see you. Were you watching me from Heaven?"

She shook her head, and in a mock-scolding tone, she answered, "Nooo, I have never been to Heaven. I've only been here and New Orleans."

It was their last day together, and neither wanted to spend it debating the nature of the other's existence, so they just looked at each other, content with their company.

Perry took a big bite of his tomato. It popped under his teeth, and its juicy insides ran down his chin and onto his shirt. Cecile laughed. He was a funny sight to see. As she continued to laugh, he just grinned. When her laughter died down, he continued to grin.

"What?" she asked him.

He pointed to her chest. Cecile looked down and saw a matching tomato stain on her own dress. When she looked to him again, his grin had grown into a wide smile, a weak dam holding back a flood of laughter. When she giggled, the dam broke. His was the funniest, most contagious laugh she had ever known. She rolled onto her side on the couch and laughed as heartily as he did. They passed five minutes feeding the laughter of the other with occasional snorts, until neither had the breath left for more. They ended with a perfectly matched sigh, followed by a full minute of silent gazing at each other.

Perry broke the silence with a suddenly sober tone, "You're gunna... *going to* leave me soon, aren't you?"

Matching his tone, she answered, "Tomorrow morning. We're having a porch party tonight with all the cousins, but I'll come in here as much as I can. Please stay. Please wait for me here."

Perry raised his eyebrows, drew a deep sigh, let his breath out with puffed cheeks that made him look like an infant, and he told her, "They're having a party here too. Mamma said she'll help, you know, with the cleaning up. I told her I can help too, but I wasn't being honest. I just wanted to come see you."

"So you'll be here tonight?"

Perry nodded his head, turned suddenly to his right, as if reacting to a loud noise, then disappeared. Cecile reached for him, but he was gone. She got up from the couch and kneeled on his spot on the floor. Her heart had traveled to vast extremes in only a few minutes. He had disappeared suddenly before, but never had it weighed down her heart so heavily.

The next day she would be back in New Orleans, and thoughts of the school year tried to sneak into her mind like a burglar crawling in through the chimney. She didn't want to think about her school or her friends. She didn't care to imagine her bedroom or the street where she played on the weekends. If she was to have only one more day of Moreauville, one more day of Perry, she wanted nothing else in her head that day, so she brought her mind back to the first time he spoke to her, when she was crying over frustrating corn husks. She went frame-by-frame through her memories of the last three weeks, lesson-by-lesson, story-by-story, laugh-by-laugh of the time she spent with the smoky young phantom who had become, beyond any shadow of a doubt, her very best friend.

She stayed on her knees in the middle of the living room until it became too uncomfortable to remain so, then she curled into a ball on her side. She was on a hard floor, not a bed, and in a dress, not her pajamas, yet she felt cradled in comfort, laying where Perry had always appeared to her. She fell asleep and dreamed.

Dreams have a way of blending what is real with what is impossible. This dream was no exception. In her dream, she was with Perry among the tomatoes. They didn't pick and eat. Instead, they played a game. They took turns choosing a tomato and describing what sort of person it was.

Cecile pointed to an oversized tomato with a deep scar running diagonally across it. "This one," she exclaimed, "was a pirate captain, but he retired with his money, bought a big house, and got fat."

Perry added, "It's a good disguise. He's so fat, nobody recognizes him."

They both laughed, then it was Perry's turn. He pointed to a tomato hanging high on the vine and said, "That one looks like my daddy. He's hanging and his face is turning red."

Cecile's pulse surged suddenly, and she could feel it in her neck. She turned her attention from the tomato to Perry. He didn't look angry or sad. He looked proud, and continued, "He tried, didn't he? He tried to get a good job. I know he would have been great. Aren't you proud of him?"

Cecile took him by the hand. She could touch him. She could feel him. She interlaced her fingers with his, squeezed tightly, and answered, "I *am* proud of him. I'm proud of him and scared for him."

They were speaking of Perry's father, but she was thinking of Perry, of how he might have died. Did he die in pain? Did he die in fear? Did he die because he was a black boy who wanted more for himself?

She turned her eyes from Perry back to the tomato, but it wasn't a tomato on a vine, and they weren't behind the house in Moreauville. They were in a lightly wooded field. The sun dropped in an instant, and there they stood, still holding hands, among a crowd of raucous men, looking up at a man hanging by the neck from the lowest branch of a large magnolia tree.

The man's bare feet pointed downward and dangled mere inches from the ground. His hands were bound behind him. The poor man was dead, or darn near it, yet the mob around them continued to taunt him. They shouted lofty titles at him, like "my lord" and "your highness".

A man standing directly behind Cecile and Perry patted Cecile on the shoulder, laughed, and taunted the hanging man, "What's that, professor? You have my attention. Teach me. I'm listening."

The rest of the crowd erupted in laughter and similar taunts. Cecile buckled over, dropped to her knees, still holding Perry's hand, and vomited through heavy sobs. When she recovered herself, she was overwhelmed by a wave of fear for Perry. She was desperate to get him away from the angry, racist mob. She stood and took a long step to the side, yanking on Perry's hand, but he wouldn't move.

He stared at the hanging man, smiling contently before turning to her and saying, "Isn't he brave? I'm going to be like him."

Cecile pulled harder, yelling, "No, no!"

She closed her eyes and pulled with all of her might, continuing to yell, "No, no!"

When she opened her eyes again, they were no longer outside, but in the living room of Paulina's house. Perry was again a ghostly image of a half-boy, sticking out of the center of the floor. Cecile was seated on the couch, holding *Robinson Crusoe* in her hand. "*No, no,*" she continued, reading from the book, "*No, no, I will carry you thither in charity, and those things will help to buy your subsistence there, and your passage home again.*"

He interrupted her, "The captain is just like you."

"How so?"

"He's kind like you. He saved Mr. Crusoe and won't take any pay."

She closed the book and answered, "No, it's not the same. You have given more to me than I have given to you."

Perry rose from the floorboards, revealing a pair of long and lanky legs beneath him. He walked to the couch. With each step, the green vapors around him dissipated. He became increasingly opaque. By the time he sat on the couch beside her, he was as solid as she.

He patted her twice on the leg, leaned his shoulder into her, and in a soft whisper, he promised, "When I become a doctor, I will pay you back. I will be *your* doctor, Cecile, and I will save you."

Cecile hummed a sigh, leaned into him, and closed her eyes. When she opened her eyes again, the dream was over. She was awake as she had fallen asleep, curled up tightly in the middle of the living room floor. Her lungs shook in her chest, not knowing whether to push forth a cry of torment or a sigh of contentment. She propped herself up with one hand, sitting on her hip, with her legs still curled tightly against her.

"What is he?" she asked out loud to the empty house. She stood, walked backward, staring at the floor until she bumped her legs against the couch, and answered her own question, "He's my friend." She sat, looked down to her knees, and whispered, "He's my best friend, and I will miss him."

Chapter Nine:
A Portrait of an Angel

PAULINA WAS THE FIRST TO RETURN TO THE HOUSE. She had an endless well of energy. After a long, laborious morning, she cleaned up, changed, and went directly to the kitchen. She had a big evening in front of her as the host and matriarch of a family Cajun porch party. The half-ghost of a severed farmhand, with his eerie green vapors, was not the strangest thing Cecile saw at her Mema's house that autumn.

While Paulina began making the roux, a man came with alligator meat and a large trough to serve the gumbo. Paulina met him on the porch and took the meat to the kitchen. The trough was not made of ceramic or metal. It was made from an alligator. It was the hollowed-out and cured hide of a large alligator, turned on its back and set on a table in front of the house. Cecile didn't know what it was for until the man set large serving spoons on the table beside it. Cecile lived in New Orleans. There was nothing like that in the many great restaurants of the city.

She watched in fascination until the man drove away. After he was gone, she inspected the hide closely. The more she looked at it, the less strange it seemed. After seeing, touching, and smelling the serving trough, she said, "It's alligator gumbo. What else would she serve it in?"

70

After three weeks in the country, it all seemed natural. It was her memories of the city that seemed other-worldly to her. Ghosts in the living room, eating alligator gumbo out of the hollowed-out hide of an alligator, visiting graves and conversing with those buried beneath —— that was life, as if Julia and Adam had never moved to the city, and Cecile had spent every moment of her life in Avoyelles Parish.

The house and the farm, with all their uniqueness, may have felt like they belonged to Cecile, and Cecile to them, but the kitchen belonged to Paulina, and the queen of the kitchen was hard at work. Cecile went inside to see how she could assist. She took her grandfather's stool, faced the counter, and chopped celery and onions, minced garlic, and listened to her Mema cry and laugh her way through a hundred stories. Before she knew it, the sun was low, and Julia, Adam, and more aunts, uncles, and cousins than Cecile knew she had, began pouring through the door.

It was a hectic scene of washing and changing, setting up for the party, and debates and arguments in a patchwork of English and French. But the bustle eventually settled. The food was cooked, the porch was decorated, and the party began.

Alfred and Nicole came last with a fiddle and an accordion. They wedged two stools in the corner of the porch. That creaky little corner was their grand stage, the point from which the liveliest music south of Tennessee would serenade the party. It was a successful harvest, but the first one without Pailina's husband, and the music captured the mood perfectly.

So much to celebrate, so much to mourn, and so many people to share it with, there was no place else in the world Cecile would have rather been. Well, there was one place, one person's company she wished to share. With every other note of music played, with every laugh and every

71

"Cawww cher", her eyes turned through the front window, into the living room, looking for those green vapors.

The Cajuns are a drinking culture. Children are offered the same spirits given to the adults. Cecile was no exception. Aunt Nora made her a diluted concoction of rum and spices. It reminded Cecile of the elixir her mother always made for her when she was sick. She drank it, and before she knew it, her step was wobbly and her vision blurry.

It would be an exaggeration to say she was drunk, but those sharp extremities of her senses were certainly sanded down, made smooth and comfortable, and like a magical love potion, the drink made everything going on around her more lovely, more endearing, and more preciously hers. She turned less and less to the living room and more to the alligator trough, the gumbo and french bread, and the company she shared.

When all remnants of the sun's light were entirely gone, she turned her eyes again into the house. She was more than a little tipsy, so she didn't believe her eyes at first when she looked through the window and saw the opposite wall of the living room waving and dancing. She stared at it as it moved with the music. Then it struck her. She rubbed her eyes clear, looked again, then remembered the promises they had made. It was Perry's green vapors that distorted the wall of the living room.

In Cecile's mind, everything else fell out of existence. She took a quick and large step her body was not ready to take, and she fell flat on her face. Adam helped her up, inspected her for injury, and sent her inside. It was exactly where she wanted to be. She walked a staggering, serpentine path to the living room couch, plopped her rear down, and looked face-to-face with her dearest friend.

Her dream had burrowed deeply into her, and in her impairment, she forgot it was a dream. She began to speak to him of holding his hand, watching his father hang from the tree, and listening to the cruel taunts of the mob. She invited him to sit beside her on the couch and take her hand, like he had in the dream.

He reminded her, "I can't float up there with you, and I can't touch your hand…, Lord knows I wish I could. And what are you talking about? I never saw my daddy hang. I was a baby, and Mamma and I weren't there when it happened."

Cecile winced in a blend of embarrassment and pity, and she told him, "It's probably good you weren't there. Who knows what they would have done?"

Perry had come in a good mood. He had no intention of spending their last moments together on such sorrowful topics, so he quickly changed course, blurting, "I wish I could draw."

Cecile didn't know where this exclamation came from, and she asked, "What…, draw?"

"Oh yes, if I could draw, I'd make a portrait of you to keep in my pocket, and when you are gone, I could look at you."

Cecile could draw, and very well. Perry had proposed a brilliant idea.

"Wait here!" she demanded.

She jumped wobbly from the couch and took two steps toward Paulina's bedroom. She turned back to Perry and insisted, "You wait here. Don't you disappear!"

He laughed and nodded, and she ran into the bedroom to fetch paper and a pencil. She came back with her supplies, sat in her spot on the couch, which had taken on the shape of her rear end with all the time she had spent there, and she instructed him, "You will pose for me and I'll draw you. Have you ever had a portrait done?"

"Me…, a portrait of me? No, nobody's ever drawn a portrait of me. Why would anyone draw me?"

She stared at him with such intensity of love and respect in her eyes that he couldn't have missed it. His face brightened as he gave her his permission, "You can draw me, Cecile, if you want to."

He began moving in circles, lifting his arms, dropping them, posing like he was holding an ax above his head, then throwing his arms in front of him like he was pushing something heavy.

"What are you doing?" she asked with a giggle, "Will you hold still?"

"I'm posing for you, you know, like a hero. What should I do? You want me like this?"

He lifted his arms high above him with his hands flexed backward, like he was holding a giant stone above his head, and made the most awkward, straining expression with his face.

"Perry!" she yelled.

He dropped his arms to his sides and stared at her, not as a hero, just as Perry, like he had many times before.

Her stern face softened. She lowered her eyes with a grin, like a mother looking at a beloved child, and she said, "Yes, just like that, like you. This is how I want to think of you. You're perfect just as you are."

Perry's eyes began to shine and glisten. His image became more substantial, the wall behind him harder to see. Cecile thought for a moment that just maybe she could reach for him and feel him with her hand. She abandoned the thought, determined to capture him on paper exactly as he was in that moment.

Like a good model, he held perfectly still, but it was not from a sense of duty to the drawing project. He was locked in a stare at her, like he was embedded in a glacier of love and appreciation. After several minutes, as she continued to sketch away, he spoke softly, "Only two people have been so nice to me…, other than Mamma, only Miss Paulie and you. But you're not like Miss Paulie. You look like her, but you're different."

Cecile put her pencil down and focused on what he was saying.

Her look invited more words, and he continued, "If God took Miss Paulie up to Heaven, covered her in all his love, and made her float in this room just for me, that's what you're like. But I know that didn't happen. I just saw Miss Paulie. God didn't take her to Heaven. She's here. You're something different."

She asked him, "What do you think I am?"

"I know what you are, but I don't understand."

"What, Perry? What don't you understand?"

"I understand why an angel would have to go to New Orleans. I don't understand why you have to stay gone. An angel should be able to get here real fast, like a snap. I don't understand why God is taking you from me now."

He still stared at her with the glow of gratitude, but there was anguish in his eyes. She didn't know what he was. She was beginning to doubt what *she* was. She didn't know why they were put together, why only they could see each other, and what purpose God may have had for this strange and Heavenly friendship. All she knew for certain was that she had come to love him. He was hers in a way that no other thing and no other person had ever been. In short, she couldn't answer his questions.

She answered him in the first way that came to mind, with a question, "Why do you still call me that? I told you I'm not an angel."

Perry looked at her suspiciously.

Cecile challenged him, "Would an angel lie to you?"

"Oh no, angels are honest."

"Well that settles it. I say I'm not an angel, so I'm either a lying angel or I'm just a girl."

Well, she had him there! He leaned forward and studied her closely, then argued, "You have that pretty, green smoke around you."

Cecile looked around her. The air was clear. She couldn't give it much thought before he continued, "... but that's not it. It's 'cause you look like one."

"How? I have no wings, no spear like St. Michael."

He shook his head and answered, "No, no, it's your face."

"Have you seen many angels? How do you know they look like me?"

"I don't know what angels look like, but I hope they look like you."

He could not have missed Cecile's blush. She could feel it radiating from her face. She had been showered with many praises in her few years, but that was the best compliment anyone had ever given her.

He wasn't finished. As her face continued to redden, he added, "And Mamma says angels are kind, and they come to help you when you need them the most. So, you see, you look like an angel, and you act like an angel. But I don't understand why you have to leave me. Please tell God you're not done with me yet. I still need you."

Cecile's uncontrolled smile widened until it hurt. Tears blurred her vision, and she spoke in a faltering voice, "Well, Perry, I will pray, and I will tell God that we still need each other…, and if an angel is just like you say, you must be one too."

It was the sweetest argument any two young people had ever been in, dead or alive. Nothing was resolved, except that they held for each other profound admiration and gratitude, and whatever their natures, they needed each other.

The party raged on out front, and it was missing one of its celebrities. Aunt Nora opened the front door and called to Cecile, encouraging her, "Boo, the party needs you. You know the family is boring without you. Come, cher, sing for us."

Cecile looked to Aunt Nora. Her face was warm and welcoming, made even more so by the flowing liquor, the spicy food, and the lively music. Perry was not the only one she would be leaving in the morning. She would miss it all. She would miss *them* all. She turned back to Perry, but he was gone. Nora walked into the living room, took Cecile's hand, and pulled her to the party.

Nora got everyone's attention. When the fiddle stopped scratching, the accordion stopped whining, the dishes stopped clanging, and the laughter settled down, and the attention of all was silently on Nora, she announced, "Cecile's going to sing us a song, isn't that right, cher?"

Encouragement came from every mouth not chewing and swallowing. Cecile's mind raced for a song to sing. Her heart was with Perry, and her mind went there too. The only song she could think of was the one Perry sang to her after church on that first Sunday. She began softly and tentatively, too quietly for most to hear. They encouraged her to sing out, so she got slowly louder.

She couldn't remember the words exactly, so she filled in what she couldn't remember with words from her own heart, and the melody was exactly as Perry had sung it. She captured the song's spirit. No doubt, it was the same soulful song of sorrow and gratitude. In her imagination, she heard Perry singing beside her.

The song contained a hundred years of soulful emotion. Mouths hung open as the entire porch stood frozen in amazement, none more than Cecile's parents. They had never taught her that song. They had never heard it in church or anywhere. Yet there it came, pouring from the lips of their thirteen-year-old daughter in deep, soulful emotion. The song struck a chord in Paulina's heart. It was like a hazy memory her mind couldn't quite grasp.

Cecile's pretty face glistened with the tears that polished her cheeks, as she brought the song to a soft, dulcet conclusion. A static awkwardness was all that remained, as though the once lively porch and everyone on it were nothing more than figures in a painting, cast in oils long-since hardened. Even the noisy insects in the field seemed to hold their breath.

Cecile let out a sigh, which, like a magic word, unlocked the others from their casing. They all rushed in their turn, hugging her, kissing her, and congratulating her performance. Once all had had their say, the party resumed. The performance moved Cecile very differently than the others. A flustered melancholy radiated from the pit of her stomach. She snuck inside alone, sat on the couch, took up the unfinished portrait of Perry, and began filling in the details from her memory.

When there was nothing else to add to the portrait, Cecile set it on the floor beside the couch and laid flat on her belly, with her face hanging off the cushion so she could see her picture of Perry. She didn't remember closing her eyes and had no notion of falling asleep, but there she slept, soaring like a pelican in, out, and above her dreams.

Chapter Ten:
A Different Ghost in the Graveyard

CECILE AWOKE ONCE IN THE NIGHT. The party was over, and only a few cousins remained. She could hear the muffled conversation through the walls. She was covered in a blanket someone had placed on her while she slept. The picture she drew of Perry was not on the floor where she had placed it. She sat up quickly and looked for it. She found it on the side table beside a picture of her grandfather.

She stared at the two pictures side-by-side. One was a photograph, clear and vivid. The other was a drawing by a child, yet it was the drawing of Perry that was more vivid, for it depicted a face she knew better, one she had seen recently. It struck her as strange to consider that Perry had died long before her grandfather, that the more recently seen face was the one longest gone.

She knew Perry was dead, and she knew her grandfather was dead. Seeing the two pictures together should have been natural, but it wasn't. It disturbed her to have Perry's picture placed among the dead, on a shrine of sorts to those who were lost. Cecile had no hope of ever seeing her grandfather again. But Perry, she had every intention of seeing him. Perry was a part of her present and of her future.

She took the drawing from the table quickly, as if leaving it there might make him fade away with the rest of the beloved dead, and set it on the floor as before. She curled under the blanket and fell asleep. When she awoke again, early in the morning, she was in the back of the family car, heading to New Orleans.

Her heart sank, but it didn't remain so. She was on the road with her parents, and she loved them dearly. They hadn't spent time as a family of three since they drove up to the farm three weeks earlier. She thought of Perry. Of course she did. But he was hers, and since he was a ghost, she didn't have to worry about him. Of all her loved ones, he was the least fragile. The farmhouse would always be there, and so would Perry. Cecile sat up, leaned over the front seat, kissed her mother's cheek, slid toward the driver's side, threw her arms around Adam's neck, and told him how much she missed him.

It wasn't until Cecile was unpacking and settling back into her bedroom that she realized the picture of Perry hadn't come with them. With all the people at the porch party, it could have been anyone's. There was no reason to think it was Cecile's, so it was left in Paulina's living room. Cecile would have liked to have it, but it didn't matter much. Perry was clearly in her memory. She could draw another, and that's exactly what she did. They ate lunch, then Julia and Adam napped, while Cecile pulled out paper and pencil and began to create a paper companion for the many months ahead.

She had no model this time, yet she improved upon the first attempt. It was a truer likeness. She drew him reaching his hand forward, so she could touch her fingertips to his. It wasn't the same as being with him. How could it be? As she drew, she missed him terribly and wondered how she would go about her days at school and at home without telling anyone about the wonderful friend she met in her Mema's living room. Yet she wasn't very sad. Perry was her secret, and her thoughts of him as she drew his image were warm and pleasant.

It was a Saturday when they came home. Julia and Adam awoke from their nap in the middle of the afternoon. By the time they all gathered at the dinner table, Cecile had begun three portraits of Perry, each showing him at a different angle and with a different gesture and expression. She wasn't satisfied with any of them. Had they been drawn by a professional, they still would have fallen short. They didn't move. They didn't laugh, teach, or tell stories.

The next day was a family day. After church, Julia made sandwiches, and they walked four blocks to St. Charles Avenue, where they boarded the streetcar to Audubon Park. To Cecile, there was nothing more romantic than riding the streetcar on a Sunday, especially to Audubon Park. She believed with all her heart that St. Charles, from 6th Street to the park, was the loveliest strip of land on Earth. The sounds and smells of the streetcar blended with the aroma of moss laden oak trees, the conversations of other passengers, and the magnificent old buildings that lined the street, to remind Cecile she was home.

It *was* home to her. She loved the city, and her flooding senses washed away any lingering melancholy. They arrived at the park, laid their blanket under a tree, and played. They began their games with *Ghost in the Graveyard*. To decide who was the ghost, they each took a piece of bubble gum, unwrapped it as quickly as they could, chewed it, and blew a bubble until it popped on their faces. The last one to pop a bubble was "it".

The bubble popping ceremony, and in fact all the rules of the game, were Adam's rules. That is to say, they were the rules Adam remembered from his own childhood. Although they played *Ghost in the Graveyard* by the same rules every time they went to Audubon Park, with very few alterations, Adam still declared them ritualistically, like they were the ancient rites of some secret organization.

The bubble ceremony always ended the same way. Cecile was the ghost. The truth is, she took her time chewing and blowing. She always wanted to be the ghost. The blanket was the base, and Cecile ran off to hide while Julia and Adam counted to fifty.

They had played *Ghost in the Graveyard* together since Cecile was seven years old, and every time since she was seven, when she was the ghost, she moaned like a ghost as she ran off to hide — every time until this time. She wasn't thinking about Perry. He wasn't actively on her mind, but he was in her heart. As she ran away from the blanket, she didn't moan.

Her image of a ghost no longer resembled the Halloween decorations or the pictures from her books. Ghosts were kind and compassionate, instructive little boys who did not strike terror in the heart. They weren't covered in sheets, nor were they ghoulish, with slime dripping from rotting body parts. They were cute, with soft voices. Their ambitions weren't sinister. They were benevolent. Without thinking of Perry, Cecile ran away from the blanket as a new sort of "ghost in the graveyard", one that more closely resembled the only ghost she had ever known. As she searched for a place to hide, she did so like Perry, with all his sweet innocence and goodness.

She chose to hide in a fountain that had been emptied for cleaning. She crouched beneath the brim and peered over the edge. Forty-eight, forty-nine, fifty was followed by Adams' deep yell, "Ollie, ollie oxen free!"

Hidden from the nose down, Cecile watched her parents search in the trees by the lagoon, around a shelter and toward her fountain. It dawned on her. If she stood up, they would see her from the waist up, much like how she saw Perry. She couldn't help herself. When they were still forty feet away, she stood and waved.

Cecile was great at hiding. Not since she was nine had they found her so easily. Julia yelled out "Ghost in the Graveyard!" She and Adam turned and ran for the blanket. They weren't trying with all they had. They hardly exceeded a strenuous jog. The point to them was to get caught, and she always caught them. Not this time. Adam turned around and Cecile was still standing in the fountain. He stopped Julia, and they watched together as Cecile stood, looking down at her legs.

They were too far, and she spoke quietly, so they didn't hear her say, "Maybe he wasn't cut in half. Maybe he has legs. Maybe he is sunk in the floor."

Of course he could be. If ghosts could appear and disappear, and walk through walls. It is safe to assume they can pass as easily downward, into the floor.

She spoke a little louder, "But why would he do that? Why wouldn't he just stand on the floor? Is something pulling him down?"

Adam and Julia had closed the gap between them, and they heard her speaking. Julia yelled out, "What are you saying, honey?" Adam added, "Are you all right?"

Cecile was so lost in her thoughts, she didn't hear them. When they were within ten feet of the fountain's edge, Adam asked again, "Are you all right?"

Cecile continued looking downward with the expression of someone who has just discovered something she doesn't fully understand.

Julia asked, "Honey?"

Cecile looked up to her parents, grinned, and jumped from the fountain, swiping her hand to tag her mother.

In a mock-scolding tone, Julia shouted, "You tricky dog!"

She dodged Cecile's hand and ran toward the blanket. Cecile ran after her mother, while Adam buckled over in laughter. Cecile caught Julia within a few strides of the base. Their feet caught, and they both crashed onto the blanket, laughing as well as they could through their gasping breaths. Adam caught up with them and threw himself on them. He devoted one hand to each of them, tickling his wife and daughter until they begged him to stop.

When they had all caught their breath and sat up calmly, Adam said to Julia, "We need to stop letting her win if she's going to trick us like that."

It is true, she had lured them in, but that had not been her intention. After a moment of silent self-congratulations for catching her mother before she reached base, Cecile considered the truth of it. She thought about Perry, picturing him whole, with legs and feet beneath the living room floor. It pleased her to consider it. She didn't know how Perry had died, but the idea that it might not have been something as violent and painful as being cut in half relieved her of a concern that had haunted her for three weeks.

As Julia unpacked the basket, Cecile thought, "He may have gotten sick, or been bitten by a poisonous snake. He may have died in his sleep…, yes, that's it. He died peacefully in his sleep…, whole, with legs, with wonderful legs."

She spent the rest of the picnic focused on her parents, but as they rode the streetcar home, she was unusually quiet and thoughtful. She thought that if Perry had legs, he might be able to leave the farmhouse. It would be a long walk to New Orleans, even for a ghost, but if he could pull himself from the floorboards and move very quickly, he could come to her. Her house on 6th and Camp had a large living room, with a wooden floor he could sink into if he wished.

"Yes," she thought, "Our living room would suit him fine."

Chapter Eleven:
The Color of Friends

THE NEXT DAY, CECILE WAS THRUSTED HEADLONG back into her life. It was Monday, a school day. She went to St. Alphonsus, an all-white Catholic school in a Redemptorist parish, in the respectable Garden District of New Orleans. The school went through eighth grade, and Cecile was an eighth-grader. She was well-respected by her teachers, popular among her friends, and in the senior class of her school. It would have been a very different sort of school year, if not for her experiences on the farm.

At first glance, she was the same old Cecile. But those who knew her well, those with more penetrating vision into her, could sense something new immediately, something heavy and substantial residing deeply within her. She participated in her classes as if she hadn't missed a day, but her contributions to the class discussions, her answers to the questions of her teachers, bore the weight of extreme thoughtfulness and the sensibilities of much broader experiences.

Her fellow students had no friends of color, nor had they any rural experiences. They certainly had never cried for a friend whose father had been lynched by a racist mob. Neither had Cecile one month earlier, and she returned to her school with a new depth of soul that hid poorly behind her petite façade.

She had many close friends, and they were glad for her return. But she couldn't help but compare them to Perry as they moved about the classrooms, hallways, and playground. Ironically, compared to him, *they* seemed like airy apparitions, silly and self-absorbed, and as thin as vapors. As the day progressed, to her friends and teachers, Cecile came across increasingly as a dark and brooding teenager, cold and distant as the stars, entirely different from the lively child that left for the country three weeks earlier.

Her friends talked about a new brand of chewing gum like it was an earth-shaking occurrence. She couldn't commit her thoughts to such things, and she couldn't share with them what was so pungently on her mind. It was not that Perry was a ghost. She could have told them that she saw a ghost at her Mema's house. That wasn't what held her tongue. It wasn't *what* Perry was, but *who* he was that was beyond explanation. She was a well-spoken eighth-grader, but she had no words to describe her wonderful new friend in a way that would do him justice. So, she kept Perry secretly inside of her, and in doing so, remained very inward.

Math was math. Science was science. The Bible readings in her religion class did nothing to reveal Cecile's changes. But then came English and *Robinson Crusoe*. The subject had already attached itself to Perry in Cecile's mind, and as the class read aloud, her thoughts were tightly stitched to him. The class was on chapter fifteen, titled *Friday's Education.* As she listened to her classmates read about how Robinson Crusoe Christianized his savage friend, "Friday", her heart grew heavier. Then it was her turn to read.

She read, *"This observation of mine put a great many thoughts into me, which made me at first not so easy about*

*my new man Friday as I was before; and I made no doubt
but that, if Friday could get back to his own nation again,
he would not only forget all his religion but all his
obligation to me…"*

Cecile paused, as if she had lost her place in the book.
Her teacher was Father Raymond, a Redemptorist priest
who was recently returned from four years of missionary
work in Brazil. Raymond had no reason to suspect a moral
conflict within his young student. He assumed that she *had*
simply lost her place on the page, and he prompted her
forward, reading, "*… and would be forward enough to
give…"*

Cecile regathered herself and continued, but when she
read the line, "*… the honest, grateful creature having no
thought about it but the best principles, both as a religious
Christian and as a grateful friend…,*" she paused again.

After a long and awkward silence, the teacher asked,
"Cecile?"

Cecile slowly lifted her eyes from the page and looked
squarely at Raymond. There was an unfamiliar seriousness
about her gaze that froze him in place. Cecile's classmates
looked at each other, not sure what brought the class to a
halt.

At last, Cecile spoke, "How can he call Friday his
friend?"

Father Raymond knew where Cecile was going with
her question, or at least he hoped he knew, and he asked
her, "Are they not friends?"

"Well," she answered, "it seems to me that Robinson
Crusoe didn't *teach* Friday."

Raymond's smile subtly lifted one side of his mouth
as he prodded, "How would you describe it?"

"I would say he molded him like clay. The teacher
shouldn't change the student, but offer the student the tools
to change himself." She added with more frustration in her
voice, "It all seems so one-sided."

Cecile's classmates couldn't understand her sudden emotional investment in the story, and a few of them jeered her. She defended herself, saying, "If they are really friends, they should learn from each other, but that's not what's happening. Friday is like a toy that Robinson Crusoe is changing to suit himself."

Cecile's point was beyond her classmates. They gave it no thought. But she was so emotionally animated, and it was so out of her character, that after a few seconds of staring, they broke into laughter.

Father Raymond slammed his copy of the book on his desk, quieting the room. When the class was silently under his command, he walked around to the front of his desk, leaned casually against it, and in a soft voice, he told them, "I was in South America. It was the 1950s, not the 1650s, but I met the natives, and I assure you, they had changed little in three hundred years. It felt like I had gone back in time."

He had the class' attention, and many stared open-mouthed, as if Robinson Crusoe stood in a Redemptorist robe right in front of them. They pictured their teacher crawling from a shipwreck, fighting off cannibals, befriending a savage, naming him Friday, and Christianizing him.

Those images were shattered when he continued, "I went there to bring them to Christ, to teach them." He turned to Cecile and added with a grin, "... to mold them. But that is not what happened. I was in *their* country. I slept in their homes, ate their food, learned their languages, their skills, their songs, their celebrations, and their traditions."

He paused in dreamy thought while the class continued to stare in silence. At last, he walked to Cecile's desk, placed his hand on her shoulder, then turned to the rest of the class, folded his arms in front of him, and spoke, "I look back at my four years with them, at the man I was before and the man I am now, and I see clearly…, I learned much more than I taught. I gave them tools to change themselves, and they did the same for me. They altered me profoundly. Cecile is right. I was no Robinson Crusoe, and they were not Friday. They are my friends, my true friends, and we taught each other. There are many themes in this book, many that we will discuss. Perhaps the first is the nature of friendship."

He unfolded his arms, turned to face Cecile, patted her on the head, and returned to his place behind his desk. He called on the next student to continue where Cecile had left off, and the class went on as it had begun, but with a strange new atmosphere in the room. The students admired Father Raymond. They took him seriously, but his words could only touch them as deeply as the limited experiences of their little lives would allow. He understood that about them.

It was Cecile he didn't understand. She had not been to Brazil. She never boated from village to village along the Amazon River, yet she saw deeply into the story of Crusoe and Friday in a way her classmates couldn't, as if she too had traveled, met someone out of another time, another race and culture, shared knowledge and understanding, learned his skills, sang his songs, and was profoundly altered by it.

Her first week back at school ended, and the deep contemplations had not shallowed in the slightest. It was the custom of her friends to meet beside the church after school every Friday and walk together to the bakery on St. Charles Avenue. They would each buy one pastry and share them all. Cecile joined them that Friday. She walked with lightness of heart, joined their conversations, and seemed very much her old self. But when they went into the bakery, Cecile remained outside. When the streetcar came, she boarded it toward Audubon Park.

Her thoughts were distant and dreamy, and she wasn't fully aware of what she had done until she was several blocks away. She decided to ride to the park, sit under a tree, and try to vividly recall every moment of her three weeks in Moreauville — every inch of the farm and house, the smell of Ti Jean's sausage gumbo, the graves, the relatives, but particularly, Paulina's living room. She wanted to recall every grain of wood in the floorboards, the green vapors that appeared with Perry, and the innocent smile and affectionate eyes of her most precious friend.

She figured half an hour in such an effort would properly affix those memories to her brain, enough to last until she returned in the spring. But she didn't get off at Audubon Park. She daydreamed right past her stop. The streetcar hit the end of St. Charles Avenue and turned up Carrollton Avenue. A few blocks up Carrollton, she finally took notice of her surroundings. She got off the streetcar. In a more lucid state, she would have immediately boarded in the other direction for the return to her part of town. But that is not what she did.

Oh, how worried Adam and Julia would have been, how worried and furious! When Cecile got off the streetcar, she saw a cluster of black students pouring onto the street from their school a few blocks up Oak Street, with a steady trickle of newcomers joining them. Cecile walked to them, among them, and past them.

She continued up Oak Street, against the flow of students. She was a white girl, conspicuously out of place among the children around her. Some stared at her, but she didn't notice them. She was focused on those who went about their afternoon normally. The things they said and did were not just normal for them, they were normal to Cecile. It was a transformative experience, as she listened to them talk about the same things as her friends. They told the same jokes, made the same plans, and relished each other's company in a way that was strikingly familiar.

She continued toward the source of the students. She turned right, then left, and there it was. Cecile found herself at the gate of a school. Teachers and parents spoke outside of the building. Students played and laughed. A small marching band gathered along the walkway to the right of the school. Cecile focused on one group of four girls, fixing all of her senses upon them. They had gathered on the street in front of the school, much like Cecile and her friends had done for years. They spoke of pastries. They added their collective money together and debated what to buy.

Swept in the moment, Cecile almost joined them. She took a few steps toward them, but they skipped away without noticing her. Her attention was caught by the marching band. The instruments began to blast random notes, as trumpets and clarinets were tuned. A snare drum struck a rhythm that didn't seem to care at all what the other instruments were doing. Cecile walked along the fence to get a better look.

She couldn't have said what she expected, but it certainly wasn't the beautiful display in front of her. The band uniforms were pristine. The instruments were shiny, and as they finally brought their instruments into concert with one another, they sounded wonderful. There was nothing very different about this school or these students. In every way except the street names, it was much like her own school, her own classmates, her own friends, much like them, but not exactly. Although she was struck by the sameness, there was a difference that Cecile couldn't put her finger on. She couldn't have described the difference to her friends. It was a beautiful diversity that was beyond words. But, oh, how she savored it! She felt herself starving for more, as she leaned against the fence.

She had almost forgotten she was so far from her own neighborhood, until a kind voice came from beside her, "Sugar, you all right?"

Cecile turned to see an elderly black woman looking at her with genuine concern. She had a large apron over her dress, with two deep pockets. She continued, "Honey, you shouldn't be here."

Cecile saw no judgment in her expression. There was no hatred and no jealousy. Cecile had been so delighted with the sameness and intoxicated by the differences of the children around her that she had completely forgotten she was in a black neighborhood, outside of a black school, where she didn't belong.

She stuttered through the beginnings of a response, and when the woman saw that nothing coherent was coming, she asked, "Where do you live? Do you want me to call your Mamma?"

Her Mamma! Cecile quickly made a list of all the possible punishments if Julia were to find out where she was. Panic overtook her face, and the kind old woman noticed. She reached toward Cecile, but she would not touch her.

"Where do you go to school?" the woman pressed her.

"Saint…, Saint…." Cecile struggled to turn her mind toward anything but the trouble she was going to get in at home. Finally, she finished, "Saint Alphonsus."

"Come," the old woman invited Cecile, "I'll walk you to the streetcar."

They walked side-by-side back to Carrollton Avenue while Cecile basked in the bubble of maternal care and kindness that enveloped her from her right. When they got to the streetcar, the woman reached into one of her apron pockets and pulled out some change. She handed it to Cecile, saying, "Baby, this is for the fare, and a little candy on your way home."

Cecile looked at her hand. It was more than a dollar, much more than the streetcar fare. She returned her eyes to the benevolent face of her companion. This woman didn't look much like her Mema. She didn't have that country Cajun accent. But she was somebody's grandmother, and

Cecile couldn't help but think how very fortunate her grandchildren were.

The woman instructed, "You get back to your people, sugar, and get yourself some candy."

Cecile thanked her and turned away, and as she boarded the streetcar, she heard the woman say, "God bless you, child."

As Cecile rode back to her neighborhood, her heart was wildly ablaze. Her thoughts were very high and low. As she left the black neighborhood, she felt herself being torn from something delightful and exciting. The afternoon had done much to transform her. The children at the school were children, not so very different from her own friends. The school was clean and tidy. The uniforms were sharp and elegant. But as she thought about the kind old grandmother, she wondered if that woman would be treated so well if she were to wander into Cecile's neighborhood. It was unlikely she would ever get the chance to answer that question, but she began to see segregation everywhere. It was a way of life she had never questioned and hardly even noticed. But she saw through different eyes after her three weeks with Perry. As she rode away from a place she would have rather stayed and explored, segregation was suddenly, boldly, and disturbingly in her face.

Behind the seats on the streetcar they had thin bars for hanging the wooden sign. The sign read, "Reserved for colored people". The sign could be moved, but wherever it hung, it marked the row of seats separating the front, where the white people could sit, and the back, where the black people sat.

While Cecile rode toward home, a large white family of seven boarded. They sat near the back. When they did, they moved the sign to the seat right behind them, leaving only two rows "reserved for colored people". A black family boarded at the next stop, then a few black students. There weren't enough seats behind the sign for them all, so they stood. They stood behind the sign, though there were empty rows in front. Finally, an old black man boarded. He was hunched, and walked with a cane. As he walked past Cecile to stand behind the sign, she scooted to the window to free the seat beside her. The man walked right past her.

Cecile turned around and watched him with concern. She was relieved when a young black woman yielded her seat to the old man, but disturbed by the realization that her gesture of kindness had probably been misunderstood. She knew how it must have looked, not like a young person offering a seat to an old person, but like a white girl not wishing to be brushed against by a black person as he passed her. She blushed deeply as she thought about it.

As the man settled into his seat, and the woman who gave it to him crammed against the others standing against the back of the streetcar, Cecile caught the old man's eye. She waved to him, which drew the look of other passengers on both sides of the sign. The man smiled at her and waved back. The young woman watched the exchange. Cecile looked to her, nodded, and mouthed, "Thank you." None of the white people in front of her saw her. Everyone behind her, white and black alike, did. Cecile didn't care.

She followed the instructions given to her by the kind old grandmother. She got off in her own neighborhood, stopped at the store, bought herself some candy, and walked home. As she got off the streetcar, she was tempted to take the sign from the third to last seat and move it to the front. She wouldn't dare, but the temptation was strong, and she thought, "Someday I will do it."

It wasn't uncommon for Cecile to socialize with her friends after school. She wasn't expected at home earlier. As altering as the afternoon had been, there was nothing about Cecile's look or behavior to worry Julia. She skipped in with her usual smile, kissed her mother, and went into her room to do her homework.

She seemed as she always seemed after mingling with her friends. In Cecile's mind, that is exactly what had happened. Her trip to the black school and her encounter with the kind old woman were not a misadventure in the wrong neighborhood. There were only other school children much like her, and a sweet old grandmother. If there was an antagonist in the story of her afternoon, it was segregation, the age-old way of life to which she had been blind, the same antagonist that forced her from the gate of the school just as she was being drawn in by it, the same ever-present villain that would have separated her from Perry, were he not a ghost who appeared to her when she was alone in her Mema's living room. As she considered this, she was thankful that Perry was a ghost, and glad she hadn't spoken of him. He was a secret nobody could take from her.

Her whole afternoon was a secret she intended to keep. The candy she bought with the old woman's money, well, that was her secret too. She put it in her bookbag, smuggled it into her room, and hid it at the bottom of her jewelry box. She wanted to savor it, to make the thoughtful gift of the old woman last as long as her memories of that day. To assist in that effort, she sat with paper and a pencil and drew a picture of the woman's face. At the bottom, she wrote, "Somebody's Mema."

Chapter Twelve:
Letters From New Orleans

LIFE IN THE HECKER HOUSE APPEARED QUITE NORMAL over the next few weeks. The changes in Cecile sank well enough beneath the surface to go mostly unnoticed. But as her arcane connection with Perry was strained further by time and distance, it began to show again. The world shared by her friends seemed small and childish to her. She began to lose patience with their limited conversations on their mundane topics.

She felt herself isolating from her classmates, and she tried to avoid saying or doing anything that would segregate her further. Her English class pushed through the rest of *Robinson Crusoe*. Cecile had already made herself conspicuous when she challenged the notion of friendship on her first day back in class. She was not keen to do it again. Father Raymond tried to engage her on that and similar topics. She thought answers that would have delighted him, but she spoke the sort of answers her classmates would have given, which only made her lonelier.

One evening during the school week, Cecile sat alone in her room. She didn't have Perry. There was nothing so mystical to enliven her days, nor could she maneuver comfortably within the tiny confines of her "normal" life.

She missed Perry in a way she couldn't understand. Their connection was unlike any other friend or familial relationship she had. She was afraid of returning to her Mema's house in the spring and finding a normal living room. The thought of moving on with her life as if nothing extraordinary had happened to her that year put a dull but constant ache in her heart.

She placed one of her portraits of Perry in the center of her floor and began to speak to it. Her imagination failed her, and it felt suddenly like a pathetic imitation. She stopped in mid-sentence, picked up the picture, and asked it, "Were you real?"

When it did nothing but stare back at her with its cartoonish features and lifeless eyes, she crumpled it into a ball, yelled out, and threw it across the room. Adam wasn't home yet, but Julia heard the yell. She went to Cecile's room to check on her, but was stopped short of opening the bedroom door by what she heard next.

In extreme frustration and loneliness, with no mind to how loudly she spoke, she called out to Perry, "Since you are dead, you should be able to go anywhere. Why can't you haunt this room? Why can't you come to me here?"

Cecile paused, biting her lips in anticipation, hoping, and almost believing Perry would appear in his green vapors and answer her. In much more fearful anticipation, Julia also half-expected to hear something else in that room, something other than her daughter. Neither heard anything. Nothing happened.

After a pause of more than half a minute, Cecile startled Julia, yelling out to Perry, "You better be there when I get back! You better be there!"

Julia's maternal concerns got the best of her. She barged into the room and darted her eyes from corner to corner. Once she knew there was nobody there but Cecile, she slowed her breaths, locked her eyes to Cecile, and asked timidly, "Honey?"

Cecile looked at her with reddening, dewing eyes and said nothing.

Julia forced a fake smile and asked her, "What was that? Were you reading your book?"

Cecile was too upset to lie. She sat hard on her bed and answered simply, "No."

The tension in the air was too thick for words to pass freely through it. Julia didn't know what else to say, and she was afraid of what she wanted to ask. She sat beside Cecile on the bed and held her tightly. The hug did much to revive Cecile and remind her of the flesh-and-blood blessings right there beside her. After a couple of minutes, she asked Julia about dinner. She spoke of food and games and homework in such a naturally rambling way that the awkwardness that had seized the room melted away. Julia was quick to bury her fears, and she pretended that nothing at all strange was going on in their lives.

Cecile's change of mood was authentic, yet that same ache in her heart remained. Had she been able to speak openly to anyone about Perry, he would have remained very real in her mind. But the longer she bottled him up the more he seemed like the memory of a lost friend rather than a friend with whom she could share her future. As the next few days passed, his image in her memory began to fade, and she strained her mind to fill in the vanishing details.

Talking to someone about Perry seemed the only way to keep him vividly inside of her. Julia was already worried about her after all the strange ghost talk in Moreauville, worries that had just begun to rest easy. After she overheard Cecile through the closed door of her room, talking out loud to Perry, begging him to visit her there, to haunt her bedroom, Julia was even more concerned, and she closed herself to any conversation on the supernatural. Her father was a loving but hard-working man. There was never a good time to sit and talk to him about her strange new friend. The next few weeks were the loneliest of Cecile's life.

Finally, an idea came to her. She cursed herself for not thinking of it sooner. If there was one person in the world open to talk about the dead, it was Paulina. She decided to write to Moreauville, and ask for advice. She wrote honestly, if not completely.

The letter read,

Dear Mema,

I hope you are not too lonely without us. I have missed you every day. I know you miss Papa very much. I miss him too, and I miss other people who are gone.

I had a friend. He's gone. I can't picture him clearly anymore. I'm not even sure he was real. I think about him, but the thoughts are less clear, and I'm afraid he will go away completely, like he was never here. How do you do it? How do you communicate with Papa? How do you keep him real? I know if anyone can keep someone real after they are gone, it's you.

I can't wait to see you in the spring. I love you.

Cecile

Cecile sent the letter on Friday. She knew it would take days for the letter to arrive in Avoyelles Parish and just as long for a response to come back to her. That didn't stop her from checking the mail every day, even on Sunday. The weekend went by, and the next week and following weekend. On Wednesday of the second week, an envelope came addressed to her. It was waiting for her on the table when she got home from school.

Julia heard the front door and yelled out, "You got a letter from your Mema." Cecile grabbed it and ran toward her room.

"Got it!" she screamed in excited response, as she closed her bedroom door behind her.

She opened the letter and it read,

My Sweet Girl,

Oh how my heart jumped when I got your letter. I miss you too, ma cher. To answer your question, I was with your Papa for a long time. I saw his face every day. My biggest fear is that I'll lose him all the way. I'm not afraid of forgetting what he looked like. I have pictures, but they don't move and they don't talk or laugh. They don't touch me or kiss me. And those are the things I want to remember.

I talk to him all day, especially now that the house is all the time so empty. Sometimes I believe he hears me. Sometimes I don't, and I get so lonely. That's when I write to him. When people are close to you, you talk to them. When they are far away, you write. When it feels like your Papa is far away from me, and he can't hear me, I write him a letter.

You're going to think your Mema's so silly. I keep a wooden box, and when I finish a letter to him, I put it in the box. When I close the lid, I imagine he has it. He can go back and read them whenever he wants. They're very personal, boo, but someday, when I'm gone, you can open the box and read them. He won't need them anymore, because I'll be with him.

Try it and see if it helps you. Get yourself a box and write to your friend. Know how your Mema loves you and prays for you,

Mema

Cecile and Paulina were similar in many ways, so if it worked for Paulina, it was well worth a try. In a closet full of knick-knacks, Adam kept an old cigar box full of drill bits. Cecile dumped the drill bits onto her parents' bed. What concern were such things to her? She brought the box into her room, set it up on her dresser, and placed one of her drawings of Perry atop it. It was as quaint a little shrine to the dead as any in the old city.

Cecile picked up one of her other drawings of Perry, stared at it, and tried to see in it the same vibrant face that had brought her so much joy in Paulina's living room. She couldn't do it. All she saw was a teenager's drawing — but then she thought about her Mema's advice.

"Pictures don't talk or laugh," she quoted the letter out loud, "and those are the things I want to remember."

She stopped straining to see Perry's face in the drawing, and began imagining his voice and his laugh. It worked, and oh how clearly they echoed in her head! His perky pitch when he spoke of something exciting, the drifting melody of his voice when he was more thoughtful, the way his rolling giggle picked up steam until it erupted into wheezing laughter, and the comical snorts as he tried to regain his breath, all came on her so clearly that she almost believed it was her real ears, those ears on the sides of her head rather than those of her imagination, that were hearing her dear friend.

As the sounds of Perry continued to ring out, and Cecile continued to stare at the drawing, the gray scratches of a pencil began to take on Perry's complexion. The lips seemed to grow fuller and take on dimension. The eyes sparkled in such a familiar way, and the mouth began to move with the sounds she remembered so clearly.

It wasn't real. It wasn't Perry, and she knew it. It was only her imagination, but it thrilled her nevertheless. She grabbed paper and a pen, sat on her bed with a book on her lap, and began speaking to Perry like they were face-to-face as before. As she told him about her time since they saw each other last, she wrote her words onto the paper. Her tongue moved quickly, and her hand struggled to keep up. Somehow it managed, and by the time she finished talking about her excursion to the black school, she had filled four pages.

At the end of the letter, her hand and mouth spoke together, "I miss you."

She signed her name at the bottom, set the pen on the bed beside her, placed both hands over her heart, then on top of the letter, still on her lap, let out a deep sigh, and whispered, "Thank you, Mema."

Each time she had something she wished to say to Perry, she sat on her bed again, listened to him speak from the back of her memory, revived his image from the crude drawing, and she spoke and wrote until everything she wanted to tell him was on paper. Sometimes she did this in the morning, after a strange or exciting dream. Sometimes she did it after school, when she had a complaint about a classmate. But she always wrote to him late in the evening, between kissing her parents and saying her prayers.

Each time she finished a letter, she folded it and placed it in the cigar box, closed the lid, and imagined her words rolling in his ears. The cigar box filled after a week, and she began to fill a shoe box. By the time the Christmas break was upon her, she had enough letters to have bound them into a book that would rival the thickness of her history textbook.

The wisdom of Paulina shone brightly on her. The letters did almost everything Cecile needed them to do. She wrote those things she could only say to Perry, liberating her to be the friend and student she needed to be at school, and the daughter she needed to be at home. She had every notion of taking the letters to Moreauville in the spring and reading them to Perry. It uplifted her tremendously to imagine it. But beneath it all still lingered the same sticky questions that attached themselves to the bottom of all her happy thoughts — Was Perry real? Would he be waiting to appear to her when it was planting time on the farm?

Chapter Thirteen:
Comfortably Out of Place

AFTER THE LAST DAY OF SCHOOL before the Christmas break, Adam and Julia always took Cecile to Mid-City. Adam's Uncle Edwin had an eatery not far from City Park. They served a hodgepodge of recipes, from simple sandwiches and po-boys, to German schnitzels, to spaghetti and meatballs. It was where they always went to celebrate life's minor successes and milestones, milestones like finishing the first half of the school year.

There was a small dining room with three round tables for four and a row of three booths along the wall. A low counter was all that separated the dining room from the kitchen. From the booth they always claimed as their own, Cecile could see through the kitchen to a service window that opened to the outside of the restaurant. For years, she watched people walk up to the window, order sandwiches, pay for them, receive them, and walk away, not any people, not all people, only black people.

In the many years they had been eating there, it never dawned on Cecile that she had only seen white people in the dining room, and only seen black people at the window. She opened her mouth to ask her father about it, but was struck dumb by the truth when it settled suddenly on her. Blacks were not allowed in the dining room. They were

104

served politely and graciously through the window to the street. Uncle Edwin spoke to them in friendly terms. He called them by name, asked about their families, received updates on their lives, and laughed at their jokes, but they could not step foot inside the restaurant.

There was nothing in the restaurant to remind Cecile of Perry, except her own altered sensibilities. She had sat in that very booth many times, looked into the kitchen, saw the service window and the exchanges that occurred there. It was normal. There had always been a rightness to it, or at least not a wrongness, until that day. She watched an elderly gentleman in a suit ordering at the window, and she wanted to scream through the dining room to him and invite him to join them at their table.

She knew who had bestowed on her this new vision. Since her three weeks with Perry, the world around her had become at the same time more beautiful and more putrid. As she watched Uncle Edwin's black patrons come and go from the service window, she thought of Perry, acutely aware of both the benefits and the burdens of his friendship.

Cecile and her parents enjoyed the meal. They savored each other's company, and celebrated what had been a remarkable year of love, loss, reunion, and newness. Cecile was not unlike herself, and it was a pleasant meal between a sweet family of three. But Adam and Julia could not have known how different their daughter was. Behind her same voice, her same laugh and signature quirks, there was a vastly expanded mind and heart. She looked around her like never before. She saw and she felt. She questioned a racial status quo that made no sense to her, and she took those questions into the Christmas holiday.

It was the tradition of the family to attend church on Christmas Eve. Christmas morning was about presents, the afternoon about games and cooking, and the evening about eating. Christmas 1958 for the Hecker Family was different. As they were getting ready for church on

Christmas Eve, while Julia braided Cecile's hair, Cecile asked if they had to go to St. Alphonsus.

It was an unexpected question, and Julia laughed as she answered, "Where else would we go?"

"I don't know," Cecile answered, "Maybe to a black church."

Julia froze in place with one full braid of Cecile's hair clenched in her tightening fist. Julia stuttered a few disconnected syllables from her mouth, with no idea how to respond. Finally she managed to say, "I…, I don't know any black churches."

Of course Julia knew of black churches, but Cecile suspected no deceit. She shouted out of the bathroom to her father, "Daddy, do you know of any black churches?"

Adam's voice projected clearly from the bedroom, "Yes, there's St. Augustine near the Quarter."

Cecile couldn't see her mother biting her lips behind her, and she asked, "Can we go there this year, Mamma? To St. Augustine? It's by the Quarter."

Julia answered without a breath of pause, "No, no, no, no, St. Alphonsus is our parish. It's where we go, where our friends and neighbors go. It's where your schoolmates go. Why would we go anywhere else?"

Cecile's reasons for the request were clear to Cecile. She thought about the school she visited, and the intense draw she felt to stay and know it better. The words to describe her motivations were hard to come by, and she struggled to say, "I just thought…, it's Christmas…, and you know, Jesus, he would… Especially at Christmas, we should…, you know?"

Julia shook her head vigorously and interrupted, "Sweetie, you're not making any sense. St. Augustine isn't our church. They're not our people. We go to St. Alphonsus."

Cecile knew that any attempt to wrap her thoughts into a neat package of words was futile, so she responded firmly, "Well, I think we should go to St. Augustine. It wouldn't kill us to meet some new people."

Adam came to the bathroom in time to hear Cecile's last words. He was startled by such firm insistence. Julia took the tone of a teacher, as she explained, "Listen, Boo, we have our neighborhood and they have theirs. We have our church and they have theirs."

Cecile added, "And we have our Jesus and they have theirs."

"No, no," Adam corrected her, "There's only one Jesus. You know that."

Cecile challenged them, "One Jesus?"

Adam and Julia nodded.

"And one God, one Pope, one Holy Bible, and one Church?"

Her parents continued nodding.

"One Church," Cecile continued, "One family of God! I think we should celebrate Christmas at St. Augustine."

Cecile's little lecture penetrated more deeply into Adam than into Julia. Her point was a powerful one. Thinking she would never agree to give up her Christmas morning to sit in church for a second Christmas Mass, he offered, "They're expecting us at St. Alphonsus tonight. We always go. But if you want to also go to church tomorrow morning at St. Augustine, we can do that, instead of opening presents."

He thought he had laid a clever trap for her, but neither Adam nor his wife understood the dramatic evolution happening inside of their thirteen-year-old daughter. A bright smile took command of Cecile's face. She bounced on her toes and agreed to forgo the annual Christmas morning paper-shredding routine to attend a second Christmas Mass at the all-black St. Augustine Catholic Church.

With ill-placed confidence in their ability to talk her out of it, Adam and Julia gave in. They finished getting ready and went to their neighborhood church, with all the same neighborhood faces.

When they got home from church, Julia asked Cecile if she wanted to help her make cookies. She had almost forgotten their promise to take her to St. Augustine in the morning. She got a harsh reminder when Cecile answered, "No, thank you. I'm going to bed early. We have church tomorrow morning."

Julia went ghost white. Adam didn't. He still believed that at some point between waking up on Christmas morning and settling into a pew at St. Augustine, Cecile would see the error of her thinking and fix her mind on the presents under the tree.

In the morning, Adam and Julia were woken by Cecile, who was already back into her Christmas dress and ready to leave the house. Her excitement matched the day, but for a different reason. She was as giddy as any child her age that morning, but it had nothing to do with presents, games, or food. As uneasy as they were tired, Adam and Julia reluctantly rose from bed and prepared themselves for an experience they still hoped to avoid.

Once they were all dressed and ready, they got into the car. Between their house and Canal Street, Adam offered several tempting diversions. Not even the fresh pastries at the bakery would steer Cecile's mind off course. Before they knew it, they were on Rampart and Governor Nicholls Street, the only white people in a black neighborhood.

It was not terribly uncommon for a family from the Garden District to drive down Rampart Street on an errand to some place or another. It was unheard of for them to turn up Governor Nicholls and park just two blocks from St. Augustine Catholic Church.

To ease the tension in the front seat, Adam, a veritable encyclopedia of New Orleans history, informed his family, "Did ya'll know Governor Nicholls Street used to be called Arsenal Street. After that, they renamed it Hospital Street, but in 1909, they changed the name again to Governor Nicholls."

1909! That's the year Perry died, or at least the year he claimed to live in. St. Augustine was just one block of Rampart, on Governor Nicholls. It wasn't much time to think about the coincidence of the year 1909. But it was enough time for Cecile to think it no coincidence at all. It was Christmas morning. Church would be crowded, but they had gotten there early and found a place on the street to park.

Adam turned off the car, and they all sat still in silence for a long and awkward minute. Adam finally took the door handle tightly, but before he opened the door, he turned to Julia and whispered, "My God, what are we doing?"

Julia responded with a sharp inhale, which she held beyond its natural lifespan and released in a slow and shaky exhale, then she took the handle of the passenger door, and pulled on it until the door popped ajar. She sat like that until Adam opened his door, got out of the car, walked around to the passenger side as if walking into the dentist's office, and held Julia's door open for her. Cecile bounced out of her seat and began to march toward the church.

"Cecile!" Julia said in a shouted whisper, "come back here and hold our hands."

She walked between them and took their hands. She could feel Julia's pulse in her fingers, and she knew why.

Two blocks is not much of a walk. They had walked eight blocks from their house to St. Alphonsus just the evening before. Eight blocks in their own neighborhood was easy with fine conversation along the way. They walked the two blocks down Governor Nicholls in silence. Other families were walking to the church, and each of them went mute as they noticed the Hecker trio. If glaring eyes made sound, those two blocks on that quiet Christmas morning would have been louder than Mardi Gras Day.

The awkwardness in the air was palpable. Julia stopped sharp, grabbed her loved ones each by an arm, and pulled them in tight, saying, "This isn't right. We don't belong here. Can't we go home now?"

Cecile wasn't without pity. She saw the anxiety plainly written on her mother's face. She intended to relieve her, but not by agreeing to go home and unwrap presents. She thought about her experience at the black school, and she assured Julia, "You'll see, they're just like us."

Julia was not at all convinced, so Cecile continued, "What would you do if a black family came to our church, if they were nice like us and they needed a place to pray? What would you do?"

Adam answered for her, "She would welcome them and wish them a Merry Christmas... We've come this far..."

He turned his attention toward the church, took his family firmly by the hands and led them to the front doors.

A few families were already seated. An altar boy about Perry's age was lighting candles. Julia looked around, and much like Cecile at the school, she was surprised at how "normal" the church and its parishioners were. Two rows of elegantly capped, white pillars ran from the vestibule to the sanctuary. Along the inner walls were plaques representing the Stations of the Cross. The lingering aroma of musky incense stained the air. The church was polished to a shine and beautifully decked for the holiday. In front of the altar was a little wooden crib with a doll of the infant Jesus. In short, it was a Catholic Church on Christmas morning, like any Catholic Church on Christmas morning.

Other than the footsteps of entering parishioners, the only sounds were the whispers of people staring at them. But the people, they were well-dressed for the occasion. The girls were in pretty dresses, the boys in suits. The women's hair was done with care. The adults genuflected before entering the pews. The little children bounced with excited holiday energy.

It was not the Hecker's church, not their neighborhood or the neighbors. But there was enough familiarity in the scene before them for Julia to take a seat. Cecile wanted to sit in the front row, but Julia forbade it. They took their seats a few rows from the back. As the church filled, an obvious effort was made by those who filed in to avoid sitting next to the white family. It was uncomfortable for everyone in the church. Children were told not to point and stare. Heads shook in whispered conversations between the adults.

The distance could not be maintained. As the church continued to fill, seats near the Heckers had to be taken. By the time the choir of children processed in, Adam and Julia were shoulder-to-shoulder with strangers, with Cecile tightly sandwiched between them. The whispered conversations were overtaken by hearty Christmas greetings between the regular parishioners of St. Augustine. The attention that was fixed solely on the white family spread to the friends and relatives that continued to fill the church.

Seated to their left was an old woman with her granddaughter. The girl, probably six or seven, leaned forward to look around her grandmother at Cecile. When they made eye contact, the girl smiled at Cecile and gave her a wave with her tiny fingers. Cecile waved back. A family across the aisle thought she was waving at them, so they too waved at Cecile and wished her a Merry Christmas. The spirit of the day dissolved the tension, and before they knew it, faces that had glared at them were smiling, and wishing them all the joys of the season.

A bell rang out, and an old, white priest proceeded up the aisle, framed on both sides by handsome, young, black altar boys, groomed to perfection for the day. Once at the altar, the priest turned and his eyes immediately caught on the white family near the back. He gave a hearty welcome to the parishioners, and a much heartier one to "the guests who are joining us from other parishes."

The mass began. Who knows what Julia was expecting. It certainly wasn't flawless Latin in rich voices. The priest spoke as if from a mountain top, and chanted as though an entire choir of monks resided in his throat. His authority in the church was absolute. His presence was larger than life. Although he was a white priest, he belonged at St. Augustine. He belonged to his parishioners. He was one of them in everything but complexion. Whatever lingering nerves still tried to cling to Julia's heart were evicted from that church by the charisma of the priest and the sense of unity he clearly shared with his parishioners.

For Cecile, it was the best Christmas morning she had ever spent. The families surrounding her were beautiful. Again, she was intoxicated by the sameness, blended to elegant perfection with a curious diversity she still didn't understand. Christmas meant every bit as much to them, as did Christ. Their faith was evident in their responses during the mass, and in the exuberant way they sang the hymns. It was the same hymns sung at St. Alphonsus, but these people sang them differently. There was a deep soulfulness in their voices, as if each syllable, each note carried a fuller meaning and was attached to a greater intensity of feeling.

Other than that, the service was familiar. The same passages they heard the previous night by Father Raymond were read by the dynamic priest. The same responses were recited. But when it came time for the sermon, it was different than Father Raymond's, as was to be expected. One spoke of the joy of Christ delivered. The other spoke of the hope of Christ still anticipated.

The Christmas celebration was joyful, but the joy, resilient as it was, had a weightiness to it that spoke clearly to the struggles of the parishioners. They were proud, hard-working people, and they wore their triumphs well, but each fine stitch of Christmas clothing, each tie around a man's neck, each ribbon in a little girl's hair was earned at greater cost. The dignity with which they carried themselves said it plainly — nothing they had came to them easily.

Cecile was not the only one who saw it. With each passing moment of the service, Adam and Julia's respect for the fellow-Catholics that surrounded them elevated, and unexpected feelings of kinship swelled inside of them. By the time they rose for Communion, they were no longer out of place at St. Augustine, not in their own hearts, and not in the hearts of the families around them. That is not to say they fit in. They were different from their hosts in many ways. This was not their home parish and it never would be, but they were welcome guests, united in their common faith, relishing each other's differences, and sharing the joy of the sacred day.

After the mass, the priest came to them in the vestibule. He asked about their home parish. When they said they went to St. Alphonsus, the priest asked Cecile, "So you must go to the school there?"

When she nodded, he asked, "Is Father Raymond teaching you literature?"

She nodded more vigorously, adding a wide smile. He placed his hand on her head and told her, "You listen well to him. He's an excellent teacher."

Once they had their turn with the priest's attention, they left the vestibule. Between the doors of the church and their car, they shook many hands, received showering well-wishes for the season, then sat down in their car, each of them letting out a concerted sigh. These were not the sighs of apprehension, like when they were getting out of the car before mass, nor were they sighs of relief, but of overwhelming feelings that couldn't find words.

When they got back home, Christmas was in full swing. They had breakfast, opened presents, played games, and followed all of their holiday traditions, but the day shimmered differently than any other Christmas. The experience at St. Augustine gave new depth to the celebration of Christ's birth. Adam and Julia looked at their daughter differently. They knew it was Cecile who gave them their new perspective and enriched their holiday. And Cecile knew it was Perry who had given it to her.

Chapter Fourteen:
An Unannounced Visit

IN THE DAYS THAT FOLLOWED CHRISTMAS DAY, Adam and Julia found themselves looking beyond the confines of their little social circle. They saw the "other" people, those who had previously walked beside them unnoticed. The beautiful diversity of their city leaped into their vision, and they allowed themselves to be enriched by it. The neighborhoods were segregated. The schools and churches were no place to find a variety of people. But there were many places in New Orleans that belonged equally to the whole city, and in those places folks of every sort mingled freely.

One of those places was the French Quarter. On Sunday, December 28, Adam, Julia, and Cecile went to the Quarter after church. The purpose was not to shop, nor to hear the music or taste the cuisine. It was a united but unspoken celebration of their shared new perspective. On St. Peter Street, near Jackson Square, there was a shop that sold bird seed for feeding the pigeons. Adam bought three small bags, and the three of them took up a bench near the cathedral.

The birds were spoiled that day. At the bench next to theirs, there was another family, a black family doing the same. They were a mother and father, a girl just younger than Cecile, and a grandmother. It became a funny tug-of-war, with the greedy pigeons as the rope. A small flock of eight or nine birds rushed to the feet of the other family as they threw down some seed, then Cecile, Julia, and Adam threw some seed, and the flock hopped and flapped to *their* feet.

Back and forth the pigeons went, and a strange and silent connection formed between the two families. They began to coordinate the tossing of their seeds, to make the scrambling pigeons more dramatic and hilarious. It became less like a competitive tug-of-war, and more like two friends playing catch. The two families made eye contact, then shared smiles, then laughs.

The old grandmother gave Cecile a wink that reminded her of Paulina. When the seed was all gone, and they had waved goodbye to the other family, they walked back to Canal Street to catch the streetcar. As they waited for their ride, Cecile said, "I miss Mema. Can we visit her?"

Julia answered, "We'll see her at planting."

Cecile protested, "That's a long time away. I'd like to see her sooner." She added in a sudden and bursted exclamation, "We can go for New Year!"

The truth is, Julia too saw something of her mother in the old woman in the Quarter, something that would never have happened before her experience on Christmas morning, and she too had Paulina on her mind. Adam had two sides to him, a hard side and a soft side. The two females in his life always knew which side was facing them. Adam was soft that day. He was open and susceptible to any suggestion.

Julia looked at him and asked, "What do you think? Do you feel like getting away from the city for a few days?"

It was a soft-spoken request, but it might as well have been a thunderous command for the power it had over Adam. His wife and daughter looked at him so adoringly. He couldn't have resisted if he wanted.

"I would love a road trip," he answered, "and I think it would be good for your mother."

Cecile interrupted, "Let's leave today! We can surprise her."

Julia responded, "No, no, she wouldn't like that. She likes to worry while we're driving. We can't take that away from her by just showing up at her door."

Adam, not the most spontaneous of men, surprised Julia, saying, "That's all the more reason to do it. Let's go home, pack up, and leave as soon as we can."

Well, that was that. They rode the streetcar home in mutual excitement and scrambled to pack the car for a trip to the country. When Cecile suggested the visit, she thought only of her Mema, but as she threw some clothes together, in a room filled with reminders of Perry, she thought much of him, and her excitement for Moreauville doubled. She packed the letters she had written to him, frantically eager to reunite with her strange, unworldly, and wonderful friend. In less than an hour, they were on the highway out of New Orleans.

They were not long out of the city when reuniting with Perry became the dominant thought in Cecile's head. Quietly in the back seat, she read her letters, rehearsed them in her mind, and strained to picture him just as she had last seen him.

The squeak of the gate to Paulina's farm was echoed by a similar sound from Paulina's mouth. It could have been any one of a dozen relatives coming to visit her. Somehow she knew. She knew it was them, and she was standing on the porch before Adam closed the gate and got back into the car.

Paulina hugged them and kissed them one at a time on the porch. Her smile was wide and her face bright, then it went suddenly stern as she scolded Julia, "Why didn't you tell me you were coming? I didn't get a chance to worry."

Adam and Cecile shared a smirk with each other, and they all went into the house. The kitchen was always the first destination. A pot of coffee was started before they could put down their bags. Pie was cut, plated, and set by the time they all sat around the table — all but Cecile. She lingered in the living room before following to the kitchen.

She sat on the couch, leaned toward the center of the room, and strained her eyes for any sign of green vapors. She would have loved to have been greeted by Perry the moment she walked into the living room. She thought of it the whole drive, but she didn't expect it. In her three weeks with him, he came and he went. Sometimes he appeared to her the moment she entered the room. Sometimes she had to wait for him. She wasn't terribly disappointed not to see him immediately, and she followed into the kitchen for some coffee and pie.

Before she did, she stood where Perry always appeared, and she whispered to him, "Perry, I'm back. I don't know if you can hear me, but…, I'm back. I'll be here for a few days…, if you want to talk…, I'm back."

She walked into the kitchen with a smile, delighted to be with her Mema, but as she entered the kitchen, she took another look into the living room and whispered again, "I'm back."

Cecile was confident Perry got her message and would appear to her when it was right to do so. She was satisfied enough to savor some coffee, pie, and loving company. She spoke little while she ate, and mostly listened to her parents talk about the goings-on in the city. Paulina asked how their Christmas was. Cecile froze halfway through a bite, her fork not yet pulled from her mouth, and she held her breath waiting to hear how they answered.

It had been an extraordinary Christmas, but what had made it so was not a subject for all company. They had attended a black church, changing their perspective on the world around them. It was news worth sharing, yet news that could not be shared.

Cecile remembered how Perry talked of Miss Paulie, how kind she was, and how she tended to his injury. Surely, if the tale of their Christmas morning could be shared with anyone, it was Miss Paulie, now grown old and even wiser. Cecile pulled the fork from her mouth, quickly chewed and swallowed her bite of pie, and blurted out, "We went to a black church."

Adam and Julia's eyes doubled in size as they looked at each other, then at Cecile, then Paulina. An awkward pause held the room.

It was broken when Paulina asked, "Did you?"

Julia began a stumbling answer, "It was…, we…, we…,"

She looked to Adam for help, who only echoed back nervously, "We.., eh…, we…,"

Cecile broke the tension, adding, "Well, we went to *our* church on Christmas Eve, and on Christmas morning we went—"

Paulina finished for her, "You went to a black church."

"Yes!" Cecile exclaimed proudly.

She understood her parents' hesitation to speak of it. She had felt that same hesitation herself when she returned from the school she visited, an excursion she still had not yet confessed. But this was her Mema, the kind Miss Paulie, and finally, she felt she could speak openly, and maybe, just maybe, tell them about Perry.

Paulina could hardly believe what she was hearing, and she passed her glances between Adam and Julia. Adam struggled to compose an explanation, but all he managed was, "Uh…, uh…,"

Pauilina cleared Adam's empty plate, turned toward the sink, and asked, "How was it? Was it very different?"

Paulina's back remained to them as she washed the plate. Cecile and Julia turned to Adam and waited for his answer.

Adam replied, "It was… the same in many ways."

He sat in a thoughtful pause before continuing, "And it was different."

Paulina wasn't angry. She wasn't appalled, surprised no doubt, but not appalled. Her reaction liberated Adam to express his thoughts, "It was a Christmas Mass. It was joyful, yet there was a heavy sort of hope."

Paulina placed the clean plate on the rack, turned, and asked, "A heavy sort of hope?"

Adam couldn't find the words, but he tried, "It was like they, well, kind of a…,"

Paulina sat down at the table and said, "Boo, I know it. Their faith is strong but burdened. It has to be strong to carry the burden so well. Poor Celeste was the sweetest woman, and caw cher, she had faith. She had a tough life before she came to us. She had a tough life after, but she always had faith, faith in God and faith in her boy. He grew into a fine man and got himself a good job. I always said it was her faith, her joy, and yes, Adam, a heavy sort of hope."

Nothing more was said on the matter. Nothing needed to be said. They all shared an understanding that none of them could adequately express. Cecile remembered Perry telling her about his father, with no anger in his voice, no indignation. The truth about his father was a burden he had always borne. That and other burdens were not like a heavy bag that could be picked up or set down. It was a part of him. She recognized it in the woman who walked her back to the streetcar, in the people of St. Augustine Church, and in her dearest friend. It was something that was absent in her family and her friends at school. It was a love that was strengthened by the weight it had to carry, faith that withstood bombardment, and yes, a heavy sort of hope.

As wonderful as this new connection of understanding was between them, the conversation made Cecile crave Perry's company even more. She asked to be excused to read alone in the living room. It was an unexpected request, but one readily granted. Cecile washed her own plate and fork, skipped into the living room, took up the book on Cajun remedies, sat on the couch, and waited.

She opened the book, read a line, closed it, and stared at the center of the floor. This cycle repeated several times before she whispered out to him, "I'm here, Perry. So much has happened to me…, Perry?"

Her heart began to sink, as she thought again that maybe he wasn't real. She considered that maybe he was a dream that her imagination had taken and gone wild with. The thought puckered her lips and wrinkled her chin. Her chest ached. She stood from the couch, took the letters from her bag, held them in front of her, and said, "I wrote letters to you. I brought them here to read to you so you will know all the things I thought about."

She let her hand drop to her side, and the letters brushed against her leg. She whispered more softly, "I thought about you. Why won't you come to me? I'm back and you won't come to me."

She sat on the couch, set the letters beside her, and leaned back, while the conversations in the kitchen mumbled on in the background. Paulina, Julia, and Adam could talk at that table for hours, as long as the coffee flowed. They did so that day. Cecile stared wide-eyed at the center of the floor, but the day had grown old. The sun sank below the horizon. Her eyelids went heavy, and her wide eyes narrowed. She awoke after dark, still in her dress, still hearing the adults through the kitchen door. She sat up quickly and looked for the green vapors. There was nothing. She whispered one more time, "I'm here." Then she fell back asleep.

She awoke one more time in the night, with a pillow placed with care beneath her head and a blanket set over her. She didn't remember dreaming. She wished she had. A dream of Perry would at least be something. If he would not haunt her in the living room, he could haunt her in her dreams. With tightly clenched eyelids, she invited him to do so. She wished it so hard it exhausted her, and she slept until morning.

By the time breakfast finished on Monday, all the arrangements were made. There were relatives to visit, both in homes and in graves. This time, Cecile knew of them all. She knew what stories would be told, what food would be served, which gravestones required a complete update on their lives, and which ones required a simple, "God Bless you, cher. We miss you."

They began in Bordelonville with the grave of Cecile's grandfather. When prompted by Paulina, Cecile told him all about her fall semester, who was getting along with whom, and all about the presents she got for Christmas. There were many lost loved ones in that cemetery, and they visited them all. So many dead people — which of them were in Heaven, and which dawdled around farm houses in a green fog? Cecile couldn't help but wonder.

She was struck with an idea. If Perry wouldn't appear to her in the living room, maybe she would see him at his grave. She broke from the family and walked along the avenues between graves, moving at pace, scanning the names on the stones and moving on.

Julia started to call for her, but Paulina stopped her, "Cher, let her explore. She's connecting with the family."

Cecile went methodically in her effort to find Perry. She found no stone with his name, but she did find one that read "Celeste Marcotte". Celeste! Poor Celeste! No, it couldn't be her. The years of life read, "1847-1870".

Celeste was black, and St. Peter was a white church. The realization sank Cecile's heart. Perry couldn't be buried there. He would be in a black cemetery. Well, as long as they are visiting the beloved dead, Paulina did say she loved Poor Celeste. She ran back to her family, driven by an idea.

"Mema, Mema," she hollered in a full sprint. She stopped at Paulina's feet and continued, "Can we..., I mean, do you ever visit Poor Celeste?"

"Oh no, ti boo, she's not buried with our people."

Cecile balled her fists and planted them on her hips as she scolded, "So, that's no reason to ignore her. She's probably wondering why you don't visit."

Going to a black church on Christmas morning is one thing. Milling about a black cemetery is something very different, and Julia told her so.

Adam, feeling differently, spoke up, "I don't see the difference... a blessed church filled with the living or a blessed cemetery filled with the dead. Who would it offend?"

Julia's answer came quickly, "The families. They don't want us there."

Paulina hummed in thought, then contradicted, "Hmmm, I don't know. We're a prominent family, you know. They might like to see us there paying respect. I think Cecile is right. My visit to Poor Celeste is beaucoup overdue."

They finished seeing each important grave at St. Peter, had a quick cup of coffee with the priest, then continued with the visits, beginning with Ti Jean. Food was served at each house — fricassee, gumbo, dirty rice, red beans - lots of red beans, fresh bread, cakes and pies, all scrumptious. Cecile had no palate for it. She nibbled here and there, and paid her compliments to the cooks, but her mind was entirely bent on finding Perry's grave.

She wasn't sure she would see him there, or if she had ever seen him at all, but finding his grave would answer some questions, firstly - when did he die? He said it was 1909 to him, but is that when he died? Maybe he died later. Maybe he died older and only haunts the farmhouse as his younger self. It was these very speculations that overcame Cecile's appetite and made her an antsy and somewhat impolite house guest.

The visits finally finished, and Paulina led them to the cemetery where Poor Celeste was buried. It was a lonely plot of land inside of a hip-high iron fence. There was no church beside it. In fact, there were no structures nearby at all. It was just a field of gravestones off of a narrow dirt road, a five minute drive from the bayou.

There was one old man in a fine suit and hat kneeling beside a stone, and one small family with two young children on the opposite end of the cemetery, whispering prayers for a dead loved one. They had to search for the grave of Poor Celeste. None of them had ever been there. Each time one of them spoke above a faint whisper, Julia shushed them, not wanting to draw attention their way.

They kept their distance from the other visitors. When the family left, they searched the graves on that side, but didn't find Poor Celeste. Cecile was no help in the effort. Her eyes sought a different name. When the old man left, they searched that side, and there she was, right where the man had been kneeling.

They were the only ones left in the cemetery, yet Julia was still uneasy when Paulina began to weep. Nobody, not even Paulina, expected the grave to affect her as it did. Memories and emotions crashed on her, as she stared at the name on the stone, and imagined the remains beneath it. Cecile wished she had studied her French. Between sniffs, Paulina rambled in conversation with her old friend and servant. It was a torrent of whiny French syllables that even Julia struggled to understand.

For the moment, Cecile forgot about Perry. She stood beside her Mema, squeezed her tightly around the waist with one arm, and cried beside her. The moment was overwhelming for them all. Even Adam dampened his sleeve with the tears he wiped away.

Once Paulina had said all she needed to say at the grave, it was time to leave. She turned to her family with a new glow about her. The effects of the visit on her were visibly profound. She thanked Cecile for suggesting it, praising her wisdom and insight. Julia and Adam looked lovingly at each other. They knew their daughter was blooming into someone special. Her decisions, suggestions, and demands had been strange lately, but the results of them were turning out to be wonderful.

They began walking toward the car, but Cecile stopped and asked, "Can I have just a few more minutes? I'd like to say a quick prayer at each grave."

There were at least fifty graves. It would take much more than a few more minutes. But Cecile was the sage of the moment, and nobody felt qualified to refuse her.

"A *very* quick prayer," Julia answered, "We are running out of day."

Cecile marched a methodic course through the cemetery, much like she did at the St. Peter cemetery, not praying, but searching. As she turned the corner onto the last row, her family saw the sorrow on her face. How could she have hidden it? There was no "Perry" engraved in stone, not a single "Perry" anywhere in the whole cemetery. When she reached the last grave without success, she was as close to crying as she could be. Her face was red, her eyes swelling, and her breaths heaving.

Julia wrapped her in a hug and said, "My sweet compassionate child."

Cecile *was* compassionate, but it wasn't compassion Julia saw. It was disappointment — heavy, pulling, deep, and dark disappointment.

They returned to the farm. New Year's Eve came, New Year's Day, and the following weekend. Cecile spent every moment she could in the living room. She swung from tingling anticipation to gut-gnawing frustration. Perry did not appear. On Saturday she sat in the car for the drive back to New Orleans, Cecile was nauseous. It was that painful sort of nausea, like she had eaten a bad crawfish.

She tried to hide her feelings, but she was no good at it. Adam and Julia knew she was going through drastic changes, changes in the way she thought, in the things she felt, in the very manner in which she viewed the world. Her silent depression during the drive home worried them. But Cecile also had a remarkable buoyancy of spirit, and they knew she wouldn't stay low very long. It was with that shared understanding that they quietly held hands in the front seat, while Cecile sat sniffling in the back, with her heels wedged up against her, her arms wrapped around her legs, and her chin resting on her knees.

Chapter Fifteen:
Coffee, Bread, and Vapors

CAN A DREAM CONJURE THINGS ENTIRELY NEW, or can it only recall what the dreamer has already known? An answer to that question would have placed Cecile on either side of the thorny fence of uncertainty, where she found herself sitting as 1959 sprang from its crib. Many times she asked herself if Perry was real. If he haunted the farmhouse and was indeed hers and hers alone, why didn't he show himself in the five days she was there for the New Year? Everything she learned in school and church told her such things do not happen. Her heart and her head were engaged in a savage duel that raged on for the first several weeks of 1959.

One thing was certain. Her perspective on race, human potential, and segregation had been completely overhauled since she arrived in Moreauville for the harvest, and if it was only a dream that caused the change, she was grateful for the dream. She would be more grateful for the friend, even for a dead friend who only came to her in her Mema's living room. She wrote as much in her letters to Perry. The more her fingers scratched the strange words into paper, the less likely it all seemed.

In the early spring, a month before planting, she wrote to him,

Dear Perry,

I don't know if you were real. I don't believe now that you were. It doesn't change how I feel. If you were a dream, you were my favorite dream. I know a lady whose best friend is her cat. If a best friend can be a cat, why can't a best friend be a dream? So I will still call you my best friend as long as you stay in my head. And if you were not a dream, if you come to me again, I will help you become a doctor. If not, maybe I will become a doctor for you. If you are only in my head, we will be a doctor together.

Forever Your Friend,
Cecile

It was the last letter she wrote to him before the car was packed a month later, and they were leaving for three weeks in Moreauville. They made it only a few blocks away from their house when Cecile's faith and doubt began to battle furiously. Faith got the upper hand for a moment, and she shouted out, "We have to go to the library first!"

Adam pulled over and asked her why. She answered quickly, "I need to check out a book, a book I need while we're there."

Julia asked, "You have your school books. What kind of book do you need?"

"It's not for school. I need an anatomy book."

Adam asked her, "Are you interested in medicine?"

"Not really," she answered honestly, "but I have a friend who is, and I want to help him study."

128

Adam pulled back onto the road and turned toward the library, saying, "Sounds good to me. Who knows, maybe you'll find a hidden talent, either in him or in you."

They went into the library together, checked out two books on human anatomy and one on medical remedies. For the entire drive to Avoyelles Parish, Cecile kept the books beside her on the back seat, resting her hand on them, and occasionally patting them like an old friend she wished to encourage. She was prepared to see nothing in the floorboards but the grains of wood. She was ready to work beside her family to help the farm. She was willing to study the medical books, with or without a ghost beside her, and if need be, follow the path her "dream" laid before her.

The same sensations welcomed them back to Moreauville — the levee rising to their right, the signature smell of the Bayou Des Glaises, the rolling thunder of the cattle grate beneath the car tires, and the familiar squeak of the gate. But the dashed hopes of the holiday visit weighed on Cecile's heart, dampening her excitement. When she walked into her Mema's living room and looked down at the plain old floor, it reminded her more of paying respects to a grave than visiting a living loved one from whom she could still hear stories and with whom she could still laugh. Her thoughts of Perry were distant, like the memory of a friend long lost.

Nevertheless, she set the three books on the side table near the couch, right in front of her grandfather's portrait. It was her first stop in the house, her first duty on the farm. If Perry was a ghost that haunted the house, even if he couldn't appear to Cecile anymore, perhaps he could make some use of the books. If he was only in her imagination, they at least looked good beside the portrait.

Once the car was unpacked, they all gathered in the kitchen for bread and coffee. Paulina had timed it perfectly. The steaming bread was fresh out of the oven. Julia sliced it while Paulina mixed the coffee and chicory. The house smelled like Heaven.

The beautifully blended aromas combined with the chatter of her family to lull Cecile into deep daydreams. As she sat, her elbows planted on the table, propping her head up with her palms, her imagination went to many fantastical places, some bright and some quite dark.

She was snapped back to reality by the call of her name, "Cecile! Are you there?"

She sat up straight, looked at her mother, and answered, "Sorry, yes, I'm awake. How can I help?"

Julia, Adam, and Paulina stopped their conversation and stared at her. Julia assured her, "Sweetie, we have this well enough without you. You just relax."

She heard again, "Cecile, Cecile, are you there?"

It wasn't her mother, father, or grandmother. It didn't come from the kitchen at all. She knew instantly whom she heard. It was Perry! Without a thought for her family, she sprang from her seat and bolted through the kitchen door. Green vapors framed the loveliest sight her young heart ever remembered seeing. Perry (or at least half of Perry) stood staring at the empty couch.

Cecile charged at him and threw her arms around him. She passed right through him and careened into the side table, toppling her grandfather's portrait and knocking the three books to the floor. She paid no mind to such trivial things. She turned in a snap toward him, and there he was, staring at her with adoring joy. She could see the goosebumps roll across his forearms and his neck, echoed in kind by her own.

They just stood and gazed at each other, until a voice came from the kitchen, "Everything all right in there?"

The voice could have been her father's, her mother's, or her grandmother's. It could have been Father Raymond's for all the attention she paid it. She hummed a subtle response, "Mmm, hmm," not nearly loud enough to be heard across the room, let alone through the kitchen door. She was utterly fixated on the wonderful half-boy in front of her.

A half-boy, or maybe a little more than half, for it seemed to her like he had regained some of his lost body. She remembered clearly that he was seen last fall from the waist up, yet there he stood before her from the hips up. It was a phenomenon for later contemplation. For the moment, it only mattered that he was there. She wasn't asleep or daydreaming. Of that she was certain. Still, she shook herself, pinched her arm, and looked around her. Oh, Cecile was quite lucid, and the glowing boy in front of her was as real as he had ever been.

Perry was the first to speak, in a voice a little deeper than she remembered, "It's planting time, so I came here. I came here every day looking for you. Then there it was, the green fog that's always around you... but no Cecile. So I called for you. I called and you came. Cecile, I'm so happy to see you."

Cecile, suddenly mindful of the ears in the next room, whispered in return, "Oh, Perry, you don't know what I've been through. I was beginning to doubt myself..., to doubt you."

"Why would you do that? We agreed to meet in the spring when you came for planting, and here we are."

It was so wonderful to hear his voice. She relished the sound more than she paid attention to the meaning. Tears fully glossed her wide smile, as he asked her, "Cecile? Why would you doubt me?"

She told him about her holiday visit and asked him why he wasn't there.

He answered, "Why would I be here on a holiday? I was home with my Mamma."

Cecile was confused. She tried to explain her thoughts, "I thought you live here..., well, not *live*. I thought this is where you stay, you know, as a..., as a ...,"

Stefan Scheuermann

"As a ghost?" he finished for her. "I have thought about this, about you and me and what we are. I have decided that you *are* an angel, but you think you're just a girl. God hasn't told you because you're a better angel that way…, you know, thinking you're just a girl."

Julia's voice interrupted the conversation, "Cecile! Fresh bread and coffee!"

Cecile stepped closer and told him, "Right now, I don't care what we are. I'm just glad we're together again."

Adam's voice rang out, "Cecile?"

"Coming!" she shouted back.

The shout startled Perry, but she explained, "My family is calling me for bread and coffee. Don't you disappear, I mean, for good. I'm here for three weeks, and I have lots to tell you."

"Oh, I'll be here," he promised, "as much as I can. I have much to tell you too."

With that, they exchanged winks and smiles. Cecile dried her damp cheeks, wiped her welling eyes, composed herself, and walked into the kitchen.   She had just been through quite the emotional moment. Her face was red. Her cheeks were damp from tears, but she glowed with joy, and her wide smile would not be reduced, no matter how hard she tried to look normal. She made no such effort. She didn't care to. Her appearance since running out of the kitchen was drastically altered, and her family quickly noticed.

Adam was the first to speak of it, "Good Heavens, Cecile, what happened?"

Paulina interrupted any sprouting response forming in Cecile's mouth, still thinking and hoping that her granddaughter was communicating with her husband, "Caww, cher, you've been crying. What happened? What'd you see?"

Cecile was overwhelmed by the heavy barrage of questions. She had hoped to sit with her family and quietly enjoy some bread and coffee, while the adults talked of mundane topics and she reveled in her glorious reunion with her very best friend.

That didn't happen. Julia jumped in before Paulina drew her next breath, "Cecile, baby, what happened? Are you all right?"

Finally, there was a pause in the questioning. All three of them stared at her, waiting for her to answer.

Cecile couldn't answer immediately. Her emotions encased her as she thought about the truthful answer to the questions. Her eyes filled again with tears. Her wide smile grew wider. Her response was choked from her throat by a giggle, forced up by her seizing lungs. There was no reason to worry. Her happiness in the moment was demonstrative, as they all waited for her answer.

Finally she gathered the breath to say, "I am very well. I'm just so happy. I missed this house and everything in it. Now that I'm here, it's all mine again."

Paulina enveloped her in an embrace, saying, "Aww, ma *ti boo,* this is *your* house, and all that's in it."

Cecile, half smothered by Paulina's squeezing arms, answered back, "All that's in it…, and everyone."

The aromas of the kitchen were the background to a sweet, tight little group hug, with plenty of kisses between them. When it broke, they took their seats at the table, all but Paulina, who did what the matriarch does, floating around the table, refilling coffee and replacing each nibble of bread.

Chapter Sixteen:
The Folded Pages

NO WORK WAS PLANNED THAT EVENING. The hours that followed their arrival in Moreauville were for treats and stories. Paulina asked Cecile to tell her everything that happened in the many weeks they were apart. An idea came to her, a clever, efficient, wonderful idea. She suggested that the living room might be a better place for story telling. It was already established that others couldn't see or hear Perry, and that Perry couldn't see or hear them. From the couch, Cecile could tell of all she had done, thought, and hoped (well, almost all) in the weeks since New Year, and Perry could hear it too.

After three and a half hours in a car, the soft cushions of the living room couch and chairs sounded lovely to Adam. He agreed and led the way. Adam sat on one end of the couch. Cecile took the other end, while Julia and Paulina sat on the chairs, as they so often had.

Perry wasn't there, not yet at least, and Cecile insisted that her Mema start. Paulina talked of the visits she had made, and of all the people who had visited her. She gave updates on the lives of every relative, not skipping a single detail, delightful or scandalous.

Paulina talked on for twenty minutes, hardly drawing a breath between stories. As she spoke of Ti Jean's plans to go to school in Baton Rouge, the vapors appeared, distorting Paulina's image to Cecile's happy eyes.

Perry appeared suddenly, as if he had run into the room. He stopped sharp and said, "Oh good, you're here. I can't stay long, but I wanted—"

Cecile interrupted him with a sharp gesture to the others in the room.

Perry continued whispering, "Oh, are they here with you?"

Cecile nodded, looking at Paulina and pretending to pay attention.

Perry went on, "Well, I can't stay. We're done for the day, Mamma and me..., Mamma and I. But I wanted to say goodnight and see-you-later. Three weeks, right? We have three weeks?"

Cecile nodded very slowly, trying not to draw her parent's eyes from Paulina.

Perry added, "It's better this time."

Cecile cleared her throat and asked, "How so?"

Paulina gave an answer to the question, thinking it strangely phrased in response to what she had just said. Perry spoke over her, saying, "Last time, we had to get used to each other, and we spent so much time trying to figure out what we were. Now we are already friends, and we can make the most of our time."

Clever Cecile waited until Paulina finished a sentence, then answered them both, "Yes, yes, that's true."

She blew a kiss to Paulina that passed directly through Perry. They both blew kisses in return, and Perry disappeared from the room. The vapors cleared, and Paulina was again before her, clear as crystal.

Once all the stories were told, and everyone was caught up on their various lives, the couch was made up as a bed. Cecile changed into her nightgown, and Adam and Julia went to bed. Paulina lingered in the hallway, just around the corner. She listened carefully for any sound from Cecile that might reveal what amazing and moving experiences she would have in that living room. Cecile could hear her breathing, and she knew why her grandmother was there. She pitied her, and she determined to speak to her in the morning, if not to tell her about Perry, at least to tell her that she had not been visited by her grandfather.

The morning came before the sun, as it usually does on a farm. Cecile slept lightly, and she was woken by Aunt Nora letting herself in. Paulina was already in the kitchen. The woman never needed much sleep. Cecile could hear the bustle in the spare room, as Adam and Julia made the bed and spoke about the laborious day ahead of them. Cecile sat up and greeted Aunt Nora. The series of kisses on her cheek drowned out all other sounds in the house.

Nora joined Paulina in the kitchen. Adam and Julia came out of the spare room. Cecile sat where she was, in her nightgown, making no effort to press on with her day. As Julia passed Cecile on the way to the kitchen, she opened her mouth to speak.

Cecile spoke first, "I'm going to sit here a little longer."

"Okay," Julia answered, "if you wish. But you don't have anything to worry about. Planting is much easier than harvesting. And if you're as good at it as you are at shelling peas, well, we'll all just sit back and watch you."

Cecile assured her, "No, I'm not worried. I just want to sit here for a while."

"All right," Julia told her, "Just remember, we can use your hands."

"I'll be there," Cecile promised.

"Should we make you breakfast?"

"No thanks, I'll eat later, with Aunt Nora, then I'll be ready to help."

Julia was satisfied, and she joined the others in the kitchen.

Cecile sat still, while the early breakfast was served in the next room. She turned on the lamp, changed into her dress, and sat waiting on the couch. Nothing happened while the others finished eating and left through the kitchen door to the outside. Listening to Aunt Nora cleaning up after breakfast, Cecile decided to join her. She rose from the couch and took two steps toward the kitchen. She found herself standing in the middle of a green mist. Perry appeared right in front of her. No doubt, he was taller. His head came up to her chest.

"You *are* taller," she whispered, "I knew you were."

"I hope so," he retorted with a laugh, "I'm half a year older."

He eyed her toe-to-scalp and commented, "And you are older, too. I can see that." There was a deep thoughtfulness about his face, and he added, "That's strange. I didn't think you'd get older. I mean…, I knew you'd get older, I just didn't think…"

She finished his thought, "You didn't think I would age…, because ghosts don't age."

"Aww, Cecile," he returned with compassion, "I know *you're* not a ghost."

"What then?" she asked.

"I'm only trying to imagine you old…, older, you know, like an older lady. And if you get old, then what? Will you, I mean much later of course…, will you…"

"Will I die? Yes, I'm sure I will."

Perry's face went pitifully somber, but then it brightened, as he said, "No, no, I don't think so. Once you're a perfectly beautiful lady, that's how you'll stay forever."

She reached for his face as he spoke, but stopped short, preferring to pretend she could touch him rather than prove she could not.

He closed his eyes and pretended he could feel her hand. When he opened his eyes again, she had turned away.

The talk about aging bodies reminded her of the books she had brought for him. She stepped to the side table and opened the top book, saying, "I brought you some books on the human body, you know, so you can study. I haven't forgotten, you know, about you becoming a doctor. Is that still what you want?"

"I sure do. Mamma would be so proud of me…, and you too, right? You'd be proud of me."

"I'm very proud of you, Perry," she assured him as she walked away from the open book. "That's why I brought you these books. I have to go outside, but I'll leave this book open, and maybe if you get a chance, you can try to read it."

"Cecile," he reminded her, "I don't see any book."

She picked it up, and suddenly he could see it in her hands.

"Oh, I see it now. Wow, that's a big book."

She looked at him with an expression of revelation, then she said, "You can't see anything in this room but me, *and* whatever I'm wearing or holding."

"I see *everything* in this room," he replied, "But the book just appeared in your hands."

"Perry," she informed him, "I don't think we see the same things."

She began pointing to the things in the room and naming them, "End table, portrait of my grandfather, chair, other chair, lamp."

"No, no," he contradicted, "The couch is there, not the chair, and the table is over there."

He pointed downward, into the floor, or beneath it.

"Hmm," she hummed as she pondered, "We'll have to figure this out later. But it's clear you can't read the book without me."

He smiled wide at her and asked, "Why would I want to?"

"You're right," she acknowledged, "We should go through it together anyway."

She returned the book to the table, stepped to him, bent down to his face, and gave a kiss to the air beside his cheek.

"I'll see you later," she promised, "and you better be here."

She walked around him and stopped between Perry and the swinging door to the kitchen, turning to face him. She reached behind her, pushed the door open with her hand, while she skipped backward with a smile, away from Perry, out of the living room, and into the kitchen with Aunt Nora.

How very suddenly she went from fearing he was a dream, never to be seen again, to knowing he was real and at her disposal! The promise of the following weeks was bright. When she sat at the table and received the plate of eggs and grits from Aunt Nora, hers was the brightest face with the most joyous glow the old Cajun woman had ever seen on the farm.

After breakfast, Cecile went contentedly to the fields. For the first hour, she patiently helped. Of course, she was not given the most strenuous and difficult tasks. She wanted to be in the fields, not running errands that a well-trained dog could perform. It was obvious that Perry thought he was working on a farm like he had in life. Cecile imagined him invisibly haunting the field beside her Mema, toiling away with phantom equipment and long-gone seeds, unable to see the living or be seen. He was unable to see Cecile anywhere but in the living room. They proved that in the fall, when they had both been in the tomato garden at the same time but only saw each other when they met back in the house.

Unlike at the harvest, Cecile knew early how quickly three weeks can fly by. Perhaps that contributed to her slowly increasing uneasiness.

She said in frustration to herself, "What a waste of time! He's a ghost. He's not planting anything, not harvesting anything. There's no reason for him to be in the field. He should be in the house with me."

She decided to convince him he was dead, hoping he would see that nothing could come of his labors on the farm. The best thing he could do is stay in the living room and appear to Cecile whenever she could make her way there. Into the second hour of the day, her eyes began to turn regularly to the house, and to the friend she thought might be waiting for her inside.

To make her escape more tolerable to the family, she doubled her efforts. She ran when others walked, carried more than she should have, and asked constantly, "What else can I do?"

"You can slow down," Paulina answered more than once, "We have a long day."

After nearly an hour at that pace, Cecile asked to go inside. She had done a full day of labor in a few short hours, and she was readily granted permission. The house was empty, and she sat on the couch with the anatomy book. Whatever it was that Perry thought he was doing around the farm, he was very busy. He had to be convinced, and she rehearsed her argument. Once her words were well-polished in her head, she turned her attention to the book. After two hours on the couch, he finally came.

He looked like he had been working. His skin glistened with sweat from a full morning of manual labor.

"Perry," she blurted in a scolding tone, "we only have three weeks."

Her outburst startled him, and he looked at her with an apologetic expression, so she softened and continued, "Perry, you're a hard worker, I'm sure, a very good worker, but nothing you are doing is helping the farm."

Perry's grimace showed his dismay. Such a statement from his mother or from Miss Paulie would have crippled him. From Cecile, it was a much heavier blow.

Perry defended himself, "They all seem happy with my work. They told me so! I'm strong, you know, stronger than any of them, and I know what I'm doing. I help the farm! I help as much as anyone else."

His defensiveness was a reaction to his hurt feelings. Her piercing compassion made her wince in pain. She stopped him, saying, "No, no, Perry, you misunderstand me. I should have said you *were* a hard worker. I was just out there, and you weren't there, just me, Mamma and Daddy, and Mema. I know this is hard to talk about, but you have died…, a long time ago. You're a ghost, and as a ghost, you can't help the farm."

Perry lowered his chin in disgust and stared at her through his eyebrows.

She continued, "You're something much more important now. You're my friend, and you can stay inside with me, where I can see you, and we can talk and read and learn together. The last two hours I sat here, we should have been together. We could have been together."

He challenged her, "If that's true, if I'm dead, why would I need to read and learn? What could come of it? If I'm a ghost, how could I become a doctor? Cecile, I don't really know what you are or why you're talking to me like this."

It suddenly dawned on him that she might be predicting his future. Chills ran across him as he asked, "Are you saying I'm going to die soon? Is that what you're trying to tell me? Are you warning me not to go outside?"

"No, Perry," she said in a calmer voice, "I'm not saying you will die soon. I'm saying you have already died. That's why you still think it's 1909."

He corrected her, "1910! You see, it's you who are stuck in time. It's 1910 now. And what about the others? Is

Mamma a ghost too, and Miss Paulie, is she a ghost? Because they see me, and they talk to me. Mamma holds me and kisses me. What about them?"

"Miss Paulie isn't dead," she spoke softly, much more ghost-like than he, "That's my Mema. She's alive, but she's not young. She's very old."

Perry brought them back to the point, "I'm not going to stop working. They'll get rid of me, and probably Mamma too, then I would never be here where you appear to me."

They stared at each other in silence for a full half-minute. His face continued to show his scrambled feelings. *Her* thoughts and feelings conflicted violently inside of her. Their battlefield was her face, which showed every bit of the turmoil it hosted.

Cecile scorned herself out loud, "I didn't say that well at all. That's not how I wanted it to go."

Her eyes turned piercingly to Perry's, and she told him, "I only meant to have you more often with me here. If you can't come to me anywhere else, I wish you would be here more."

An idea came to Perry, and he told her, "I could work twice as hard, twice as fast. Then they would let me rest more often and let me come inside and help Mamma with the house work."

Cecile blurted, "That's what I did this morning!"

"You helped with the house work?"

"No, I worked twice as hard so I could come inside sooner. Perry! That's a great idea."

Having so quickly won back her approval pleased him, and he bounced up and down on toes that weren't there.

She apologized for hurting his feelings, informing him, "Perry, you don't know what I've been through. I'm sure you never lose faith, but I did. Shame on me, I did. I wish you could have seen me—"

She interrupted herself, remembering the letters she had written to him. "Wait here!" she gruffly whispered before bolting into the spare room and rummaging through her bag for the letters.

He was dutifully waiting for her when she returned to the living room. His eyes went from her face to the letters he could clearly see in her hand.

"I wrote to you," she told him, "I missed you so much, and I wrote you letters."

Cecile kneeled down on the floor, shoulder-to-shoulder with her friend. He read what he could read. She helped him when he needed help. As they read together all her written expressions of love, friendship, loss, and doubt, he moved his fingers caressingly across her shoulders, occasionally passing his hand right through her. It didn't matter much that they couldn't feel the other's touch. What they *did* feel, those matters of the heart, they felt intensely.

His reading had improved in their months apart. Cecile thought it strange and wondered how he could have practiced without her, since he couldn't see the books on the bookshelf. She asked him and he answered, "Our book, *Robinson Crusoe*, I found it on the shelf and I've been reading it. Miss Paulie said I could read whatever I wanted. She was surprised I could read. You know, I couldn't before, then suddenly I could read. She doesn't know about you, that you appeared to me and taught me to read. She thinks I'm just smart..., very smart."

"You found *Robinson Crusoe*? And you read it? I thought you couldn't see the things in the room. How?" she asked him, wondering if it was the very same copy.

"I couldn't see the book you had, unless you were holding it, but I found it here on the shelf," he answered, "I have read it. When I got to a part where I need help, I folded the page, so you could help me when you come back. See?"

He moved to a blank part of the wall, reached forward, and a copy of *Robinson Crusoe* appeared ghostly in his hand. It sure looked the same. Cecile went to the bookshelf and took up her Mema's copy. It was just as she remembered it, worn and well-used, with many pages folded at the upper corner.

Perry opened the copy he had to a folded page in the seventh chapter, and he showed her, "See? I folded this page because there are parts I don't understand."

Cecile turned her book to the same page. It too was folded, exactly how and exactly where Perry had folded it. It was clearly the same book.

"This is strange," she told him. "The book is…, this can't be."

"What do you mean?" he asked.

"I remember this fold. It was like this before…, last year. I wonder who folded it. Maybe Mema folded the pages. These pages couldn't have been folded by you. You didn't start reading it until after I met you, after you…, after you were already a—"

"No, *I* folded the page," he reminded her, "I just told you that. None of them were folded until I did it."

"None of them?" she snapped, "You mean there were no folded pages when you started reading it."

Through a confused smile and furled eyebrows, he reminded her, "I said that already."

"I know, I know," she responded in a fog of wonder, "but, but, that was after you…, after you… How…, how…? It must have been Mema."

"Cecile," Perry interrupted, "I'm glad He sent *you* to me, but you must be the strangest angel. I told you I folded the pages. Why are you surprised that they are folded? Why wouldn't they be? You aren't mad, are you, about the pages? I can unfold them."

"I'm not mad," she assured him, "only confused. Tell me again quickly, when you folded the pages, were other pages folded?"

"No," he answered innocently, "It was like new. Was it bad of me?"

"No, no," she assured him, "I'm just a little…"

She turned the pages to the next folded page. He did the same. It was the same page, the same fold, undeniably the same book. The mystery began to overwhelm her. It was too much to consider. She put the enigma behind her and set her mind to teaching. They worked together through the difficult passages until he could read them smoothly.

Dinner was to be served soon. They both had to leave the living room, but before they did, he told her, "I used to think we were like Robinson Crusoe and Friday, but I don't think that anymore. You're not at all like Robinson Crusoe. No, we are much better friends."

She smiled softly, and a thoughtful wrinkle formed on her chin, as she told him, "I agree. They were never friends, not real friends. And I never saw myself as Robinson. I saw myself more like Friday. When you taught me how to husk corn and shell peas, I felt like Friday, but *we* really love each other. I don't think they did."

"Exactly!" he exclaimed with a bright face.

She blew him a kiss. He caught it in his hand, then disappeared.

Chapter Seventeen:
From the Castaway to the Skeleton

THE MYSTERY OF THE FOLDED PAGES put a constant itch in the inside of Cecile's skull that could only be scratched with answers. It was dinner time with Cecile, where she had built a reputation for strange questions that seemed to come from nowhere, so it surprised nobody when she blurted out of the blue, "Mema, what have you been reading?"

"Cher," Paulina answered, "I've been reading the Old Testament before bed, and lately, I like to read poetry. Nora bought me Charles Boudelaire. I like reading in French, reminds me of my Daddy."

She continued, "What about *Robinson Crusoe*? Have you ever read that?"

Paulina puckered her lips as a wave of emotion washed over her. She rolled her head in a circle, hummed softly, then answered, "No, boo, that was my father's book. He was determined to read it, but he never got around to it. No, it's been sitting lonely, I'm afraid. It sat untouched and like new for years. But somebody read it years ago, maybe one of the cousins. It sure looks well-loved now. Poor, worn-out old thing."

"But Mema," Cecile challenged, "many of the pages are folded. Do you remember anyone doing that."

"No, no, Sweetie, it's been an old used book a long, long time now. I don't remember anyone reading it, but someone sure loved it. Part of it's charm, I think."

Julia, lost as ever in such conversations, dared an opinion, "I agree, Mamma, I love an old worn book, with dog-eared pages and faded inscriptions to people long gone. I like to think about who had held it, and who loved it."

"Yes," Paulina added, "that old book sure does look loved. I wonder who has read it."

These were dreamy thoughts Cecile had no mind for. She knew who read it. Her questions were more practical. Perry claimed to have folded the pages after they met in the fall, but Cecile remembered those same pages already being folded when she first read the book to him. How? How in Heaven's Name could Perry have worn and folded the pages of a real book after he had died, after he was a ghost?

Thinking aloud, she asked, "Can a ghost change things about the past?"

The mention of ghosts seemed to come out of nowhere to the others at the table. Julia didn't hide her concern well. More ghost talk! She let out a sigh with a slightly vocalized hum. Adam's concern was more for his wife than his daughter. To soothe the air, Paulina seized a serving dish and made her normal pass around the table, refilling each space on each plate.

Adam wanted her to elaborate, and he asked frankly, "What do you mean, honey?"

Far more focused on her mission than her appearance, Cecile answered, "If a ghost…, a person who has died, does things, you know, touches things…"

Paulina finished for her, "Can ghosts move things around, like chairs and such?"

"No, no," Cecile corrected, "I mean if they touch things, like a book, and they think they're still living in their own time, can it change…, you know, can it…"

She was clearly frustrated and confused, and deeply affected.

Paulina tried to prompt her forward, "Go on, can it what?"

"Mamma, no!" Julia interrupted, "She's upset. Enough of this. Let's talk about something else."

Paulina kissed Cecile's head and agreed, saying, "Maybe your Mamma's right, cher. Sometimes there's no answers. We just have to go on faith. Spirits live in eternity. Who knows what they can or can't do?"

"Mamma!" Julia scolded, "Something else!"

Adam relieved the tension by interjecting some trivial comments about his job. Once on that track, the conversation moved naturally onto topics less distressing to Julia. The rest of the dinner was quite normal, at least in appearance, but questions and concerns had burrowed into the hearts of each one of them, and remained there throughout the meal, leaving a residual strain in the savory air.

After dinner, they all returned to the fields, all but Cecile, who was given duties nearer to the house. She gathered eggs, cleaned the coop, and cut the old tomato vines. It took her about two hours. She moved at top speed, and when she had done all that was assigned to her, she cleaned up, changed clothes, and went directly to the couch.

She didn't wait long for Perry. But rather than appearing upright, like he normally did, he rose out of the floor, as if he had been crouched down, hiding beneath the floorboards. He had a cloth in one hand and a jar of oil in the other.

"Perry?!" Cecile squealed in startled delight.

"Oh, Cecile," he spoke rapidly, "you will be so happy. I had an idea, you see. I told them I hurt my knee. I hated to tell a lie, but it's a good lie. The floors needed to be oiled, the floors and sideboards, and the bookshelves, the table and chairs, and all the wood. So I said I could do it. They agreed! Now I get to work in the house, at least for a couple days."

It *was* good news, but Cecile was focused on the enigma of the pages. She interrupted him, "Perry, quickly, get the book, *Robinson Crusoe*. Get it now."

Perry obeyed, and in three seconds he stood before her with it ghostly in his hand.

Cecile flipped through the book to a random unfolded page, instructing him, "Turn to page…, sixty. Go to page sixty."

Perry did as she asked, and waited for further instructions.

"Now fold it. Let me watch you fold it."

He did as she said.

"No, no, sorry" she stopped him, "not sixty, that one is already folded. Go to page…, seventy-three, yes, fold that one."

He obeyed.

Shaking and speaking in a frantic voice, she said, "No, sorry, that one is already folded too. I need to…"

"Shhh," he calmed her, "Cecile, what's wrong?" After a pause, he continued, "Oh, I see. Don't try to figure it out. That's God's job. We just have to go on faith."

It was word-for-word what Paulina had told her, and it rang in her mind, closing her lips and slowing her breath. In a haunting tone, she repeated, "We have to go on faith."

"Yes," he encouraged her, "Whatever we are, this is strange, strange and special. We were put together by God."

She added, "… for your benefit or mine?"

"… or both," he said with a smile.

The thought of benefitting Perry reminded her of the books she had brought with her. She took up the first anatomy book, kneeled on the floor beside him, opened the book, and said, "I guess we should get to work. Here look."

Cecile was an excellent reader, but she knew little of human anatomy. Their shared struggle with the funny-sounding names in the book spawned awkwardness and laughter.

As they worked their way through the bones of the arm, Cecile stopped reading, raised an eyebrow in a confused stare at the book, and said, "This can't be right."

"What?" he begged her, "What can't be right?"

She lifted her eyes from the book to him, weakly fighting back a smile, and she answered, "This bone in the wrist, it must be mad at the other bones."

"Why?" he coaxed her, "Is it smaller..., less important?"

"I don't know why, but it's definitely angry. It's called the pisiform bone..., pissy form, get it? Pissy - form!"

Aparently "pissy" was a word he didn't know, not as she knew it. She explained the slang term to him, adding it eternally to his vocabulary. Once the comedy of the bone name was fully understood by both, they spent the next twenty minutes speculating together what could have happened to the pisiform bone to put it in such a foul mood. Perry suggested that the other bones slept, and the pisiform bone had to do all the work on the farm. Cecile said that all the bones in the body celebrated their shared birthday, but forgot to invite the poor little pisiform bone.

On and on the theories came, each resulting in a new eruption of laughter. Class time was over! Cecile stopped being a teacher, but oh, how they laughed! Once they had their fun with the pisiform bone, Cecile stopped working her way through the arm in orderly, scholarly fashion. She looked only for funny sounding names, and the human body has plenty of them. And that is how they ended their day, pitting bone against bone in hilarious family drama, creating romances between ligaments and organs, and assigning the quirkiest personality traits to muscles and blood vessels.

Robinson Crusoe had nothing on the wild fictions they created with the book on human anatomy. It was a game, meant to be funny, to make the other laugh, but it served a hidden purpose. Each little story associated with a body part, each nickname, every little make-believe conflict they set raging in the human body cemented the names in their memories. Neither would ever forget the angry little pisiform bone, where it was in the body, or how the other bones of the wrist made it so mad. The best professors in the greatest medical schools in the country could have learned from those two silly children and their silly little game.

The day ended. The rest of the family came inside. Perry disappeared and took his green vapors with him. Left behind him were delightful memories of an afternoon of fun and laughter with Cecile's very best friend, and an admirable knowledge of human anatomy.

Perry's faked injury gave them many hours together. His studies enjoyed all the benefits of Cecile's genius mode of teaching, though accidental. They worked their way through the books she had brought, learning of diseases and medicines, and the various functions of the body. It was all funny. It was all a game. When they got to human reproduction, not even that was awkward. It was scientific and comical. Like the rest, they made a game of it.

It wasn't all bones and ligaments. Perry's little lie gave them time for stories of their time apart. They spoke openly about their hopes and fears, and they spoke honestly and regularly about their growing love and appreciation for each other.

When the weeks of planting were over, and it was time to return home, Cecile was at ease. She left with new knowledge and wisdom, a remarkable medical understanding for a child her age, but also something much more profound. She need never again doubt that Perry was real, not just a dream or a figure she created in her wild imagination. They never got to the bottom of the folded page mystery. They never spoke of it again. They were content to place it among the many other mysteries of their extraordinary friendship.

She knew he wouldn't appear to her in New Orleans, and that she would have to live without him until she came again to Moreauville. But they had grown much closer in those three weeks. She left the farm knowing he would be there. He would *always* be there, and she was determined to spend more time at her Mema's farmhouse, in that wonderful and magical living room, with the most unlikely best friend a girl ever had.

Chapter Eighteen:
The Summer of Dancing and Candles

BACK IN NEW ORLEANS, CECILE KEPT PERRY close to her heart. She continued to write him letters, with the intimate details of her life that a teenage girl only shares with her dearest of friends. Every triumph and failure, every boy she thought was cute, every new friend gained and old friend lost made it into her letters to Perry. But such details were only the beginning of each letter. They ended with another body part, some other heroic bone and its wild misadventures. In short, she continued the game they had created together, and couldn't wait to share it with him the next time she was in Moreauville.

Before meeting Perry, Cecile never had an interest in visiting the country, so it didn't occur to Julia and Adam to offer her a special trip outside of the laborious three weeks in the spring and the fall. It didn't occur to Julia or Adam, but it did occur to Cecile. During the last week of school that spring, as they discussed over dinner the summer plans of her friends, Cecile asked to visit Paulina.

Adam warned her, "The summer days can be boring in the country. It's too hot to play outside for very long.

You'll be stuck inside for hours, with nothing to do but read."

Nothing sounded sweeter to Cecile. She had friends at school, and she loved them dearly, but an inexplicable chord of connection bound her soul to Perry. There was something Providencial in their friendship. They had been put together by God, for some reason only God knew. Her desire to be with Perry came from something much deeper than friendship, dictated by something greater than affection. Long hours stuck inside with Perry was the best description of a perfect summer, and her face lit up as Adam spoke.

Julia thought of her lonely mother, alone in the old home of her marriage. She immediately supported the idea, saying, "I think it would be good for you and your Mema to spend a few days alone together."

"A few days?" Cecile protested, "I was thinking…, I don't know…, maybe a month?"

Adam raised his eyebrows and questioned, "A full month away from your daddy? Don't be cruel."

Cecile explained, "For all those years since I was six, I hardly saw her. Now I'm older. I'm not a burden. Wouldn't it be good for us to spend time together?"

Julia suggested, "A full month with her granddaughter, Mamma would love it."

"Well," Adam relented, "it seems I am out-voted. But you had better write me letters."

Thoughtlessly excited, Cecile blurted, "I will. I'm very good at writing letters."

"When do you write letters?" Julia asked, "... and to whom?"

Cecile froze in place as she scrambled internally for an answer she could give honestly. After a pause, she said, "I've written to Mema, and I write stories with letters in them."

The crisis seemed averted, until Adam told her, "I didn't know you wrote stories. I'd love to read them."

Her claim wasn't untrue. She did make up stories. The Dramatics and Adventures between the Parts of the Human Body, by Cecile Hecker and her ghostly friend Perry, was a grand book in the making.

"You can read it someday, Daddy," she told him, "It's a work in progress."

Adam was content, and he yielded to the plan. Cecile would spend the month of July with her Mema in Moreauville — and with her very dearest friend.

Julia was right. Paulina was delighted to have her granddaughter, and for a whole month alone..., almost alone. They spent most of their time together in the living room or the kitchen. Perry had no injury to fake. He made his appearances for 10, 15, 20 minutes at a time before having to return to work. Cecile got used to sharing the company of two people who couldn't see or hear each other. Perry enjoyed standing quietly, watching and listening to Cecile talk with her Mema. He learned much about her life, and about her dreams for the future.

Cecile would often repeat Paulina's questions before answering them, so Perry knew what she was talking about. Paulina thought it odd, but it came from Cecile's mouth, where odd was quite normal. Cecile missed her parents. She missed the picnics in the park. But she had never passed a more blissful month.

When it was quiet time, and Paulina sat and read or knitted, Cecile read out loud from medical books she had brought with her. She answered Perry's questions when she could do so without raising an eyebrow from Paulina, and together they continued to make up silly stories with the funny names in the book. The quiet time in the living room with Paulina was also the perfect time for Perry to talk to Cecile. When her eyes could stare at no more letters on a page, she simply listened. It was in those times, hearing

155

him ramble on about his mother, his work on the farm, his ambitions, what he thought was wonderful and what he thought was tragic, it was in those times she came to truly understand what a kind, beautiful, and special boy he was.

One afternoon, Paulina asked her, "Cher, you're all the time reading that book. I didn't know you wanted to be a doctor."

"Me?" Cecile answered, "No, not me. I want to be a story-teller, and make up stories about angry little bones." Keeping her face pointed at Paulina, she turned her eyes to Perry and gave him a wink.

One afternoon, the large fan broke down. The shade of the house offered little more comfort than the heat of the fields. Paulina made a large pitcher of sweet tea and brought the whole thing into the living room, along with a large bowl of ice and two tall glasses. It was too uncomfortable for knitting or reading. Cecile and Paulina, their garments sticking to their sweaty skin, lounged back on the couch together and cooled themselves from the inside out with the frigid tea.

As the sun went lower and the house cooled slightly, Paulina recovered enough to transition from slouching and panting to sitting upright and singing. She sang an old French children's song. Cecile only picked up a few of the words, but the melody was catchy and repetitive, and Cecile soon contributed by humming along. Maybe it was coincidental timing, or maybe Perry was beckoned by her voice. He appeared within a few seconds of Cecile's first note.

Of course, he couldn't hear Paulina, but he heard Cecile, and he stood listening and staring at her. His face went contemplative. He gave her a gentle nod of his head, then extended his hand to her. She continued to hum along with her Mema, as she stood and walked to him. Perry reached his other hand and began to sway to her voice. She closed the little space between them, until they were against each other. Had they been able to touch, they would have been pressed together in a tight embrace.

Cecile began to sway in time with him. She interlocked her fingers behind his neck — and they danced. It didn't matter to her that she could see her own hands through him, or that he rose only chest high to her. He didn't care that he couldn't rest his hands on her waist. They danced! And Paulina delighted in watching her granddaughter dancing to the song. They were quite the trio, Cecile, Perry, and Paulina.

The next day, Cousin Alfred came to the house and repaired the fan. He brought a gift for Paulina. It was a record player, a broken one he had repaired and brought back to life. Along with the record player, he gave two records, a compilation of big bands and a record by Fats Domino. Paulina knew what she wanted to hear first. The sweet voice and rolling piano of the New Orleans native filled the living room from floor to ceiling.

That afternoon, and every afternoon for the rest of Cecile's visit, there was music and dancing. They danced fast. They danced slowly. To Paulina, it was a dance for two. She didn't see, hear, or sense the third member of their party. When Cecile sang along, Perry danced to music, but he couldn't hear the record player. When she didn't sing, he danced to the rhythm of her movements. He needed no more accompaniment than that. Without lamenting out loud, both Perry and Cecile regretted their inability to touch each other. The dancing bonded them in a new way, but they couldn't take each other's hands. She couldn't rest her arms on his shoulders. And he couldn't take her by the waist.

To Cecile, it was both the quickest and the longest month she could remember. It seemed to go by in a flash, but it was filled with more love, new understanding, and tightening of bonds than a normal person could fit into a year. When Adam and Julia came to take her home, she felt

157

high, like she always felt on Christmas night after sipping her father's Glühwein. She said "I love you" to her Mema and to her best friend in the same breath, knowing she would see them both in a few short months.

Back home in New Orleans, she told her parents about her visit, speaking of all the wonderful time she spent in Paulina's living room. Of course, she didn't speak openly of Perry, but with creative vagueness, she even found a way to talk about the time she spent with him.

After a month apart, Cecile and her parents were in need of some quality time together. On the last weekend of the summer break, they made a very special trip. This was an outing reserved for the most momentous occasions. The only occasion this time was love. They went to Biloxi, Mississippi. In the early 1950s, the U.S. Army Corps of Engineers imported beautiful white sand and created a beach to protect the Mississippi seawall from the hurricanes that battered the coast. The new beach did much more than that. It drew vacationers from Louisiana. Well, it drew white vacationers. Black people were not yet allowed on the Biloxi beaches.

After an hour and a half drive, filled with singing and laughing, they checked into the luxurious Edgewater Hotel, on the beautiful white sands of the Biloxi Beach. Trips to Biloxi were unlike any other trips the Heckers took. They spared no expense, and Cecile was made to feel like royalty. They awoke on Saturday morning, ate a delicious breakfast, went to the shops to buy them all new swimsuits and beach toys, and were on the sand by 9:30 am.

Adam had an idea beyond sandcastles and swimming, an idea he hatched before they left. He purchased a portable gas stove from the army surplus store and brought it, along with a block of wax, some string, and an old pot. His intention was to make special souvenirs of their trip. While the ladies waded into the water, Adam dug a small pit in the sand. He heated the wax in the old pot, over the flame of the gas stove, then called for his wife and daughter.

Adam went first. He poured the hot wax into the pit in the sand and sank the string into it. Cecile didn't know what he was doing. Julia figured it out and began digging her own pit.

"Candles," she told Cecile, "We are making sand candles."

Cecile dug her own little pit in the sand. She intended it to be shaped like a star. It looked more like a squid that had washed ashore. Adam poured hot wax into their holes, and Julia and Cecile added their own wicks. They left the candles to harden and waded into the water together.

As they splashed and played, the beach began to fill with other vacationers and locals. Cecile enjoyed watching the other families having fun. She went back onto the sand to make a sand castle and delight in the joyful faces around her. She gave no thought to the fact that they were all white, until her ears were drawn to a small crowd gathering on the road. Adam told her they were black protesters, peacefully protesting their exclusion from the public beach.

It drew her attention back to the people on the beach, to the ones playing ball and flying kites, making castles and swimming, all of them white as the sand they were enjoying. Cecile grinded her teeth in anger, but she didn't know who should receive her anger. It wasn't the people on the beach. Afterall, she and her parents were white people on the beach. Not knowing where to direct her anger made the feelings all the more intense.

Adam and Julia forced her attention toward the purpose of the trip — to enjoy each other's company before the new school year separated them. They returned to their sand candles. The wax had hardened, and they pulled the candles from the sand. Each was encrusted with a shell of Biloxi sand. Such a marvelous idea, a wonderful invention, and a novel souvenir!

Cecile's squid-shaped candle was as special to her as it was unique among all candles in the world. She took her candle to the gathering of protesters. She was halfway there before Adam and Julia knew she had left them. They ran in pursuit and reached her just as she drew the attention of the protesters. They had learned enough of her wisdom to wait and see what she would do.

Cecile walked to an impassioned young man. He was angrier than the rest, and wore a scowl to show it. He turned to Cecile, who was as sand-encrusted as her candle. She was framed from behind by her parents as she handed the young man her candle and told him, "Here, this is for you. It's part of the beach, and you should have it."

The man took the candle, and his features softened. His scowl turned to a warm smile. Whispers waved across the gathering, and Julia, the same woman who had been terrified to get out of her car on Christmas morning, teared up with pride in her daughter. She ran back to their little part of the beach and returned with hers and Adam's sand candles. Julia and Adam followed Cecile's example and ceremoniously presented the protesters with a little part of the Biloxi beach.

Their actions drew the attention of the vacationers. Most of them had no idea what was happening, and they didn't care. Nevertheless, the Heckers packed up their things and returned to the hotel. On Sunday, they went to a different part of the beach. They had no more wax for candles. Even if they had, they wouldn't have made more. In their minds, it would have cheapened their gifts to the protesters. Sand candles would have to be a souvenir of the next summer, and the many that followed after. They returned to their home on Sunday evening with only their new swimsuits, new beach toys, and an ever-clearing vision of the world around them, of what is beautiful and what is not, what is just and what is unjust.

Chapter Nineteen:
The Man in the Suit

THE TIME UNTIL THE HARVEST WENT AS IT OFTEN DOES when someone is eagerly anticipating. Like the last few days before Christmas, each day felt like ten. Cecile couldn't have said how or why, but she expected some revelation from this visit to Moreauville. She just knew it was coming, and she strongly suspected it had to do with Perry.

Adam drove them there early and had to leave immediately to get back home. He had an important meeting the next day. Cousins were already on the farm helping Paulina. Julia set down her things and joined them in the fields, leaving Cecile alone in the house. She waited, read, drew, wrote, and repeated that cycle several times before the kitchen crowded with family gathering for dinner.

It had been a particularly hot morning, and the early afternoon was not cooling one degree. When Cecile joined them, hers was the only face not deeply reddened and glistening with sweat. Paulina seemed more done-in than the others. She stood by the sink and drank a tall glass of water, refilled it, and drank it down again.

It was a simple dinner that day, just a large dutch oven of red beans and a pot of rice. Being the only one feeling quite well, Cecile offered to serve. Paulina thanked her and took a seat at the table. It was the first time anyone could remember Paulina sitting at that table while another served, and Cecile was honored to step into those shoes. There was more eating than talking. It was not a very Cajun sort of dinner. It was more business than pleasure, like the German meals of Adam's childhood household.

After the meal, when the cousins returned to the fields, Paulina stayed behind to clean up. She appeared increasingly unwell. The food, water, and rest had not recovered her at all. Julia commanded her to go to bed. But a Cajun woman is the master of her household, and Paulina felt bad enough about being unable to serve at the table. She insisted on cleaning, but welcomed Julia's help.

Cecile helped wash the dishes. Once they were all cleaned, and they only needed to be dried and put away, Julia asked her to help the cousins outside.

"Oh no, cher," Paulina protested, "It's too hot. We have enough without her."

"We have one less," Julia insisted, "You're not going back out there until you look much better. You're going to bed. That's an order."

Cecile agreed, "I think you're right about that, Mamma."

"Well," Paulina submitted, "When you two team up, I don't stand a chance."

Paulina insisted on finishing the cleaning before going to bed. Julia stayed to help her and sent Cecile to the living room. It was where she wanted to be, to wait as long as she must for Perry. She had hardly finished folding her legs beneath her on the couch when he appeared. They grinned and winked at each other. Cecile got up, walked to him, and leaned forward to give him a kiss.

While Perry's green vapors filled her eyes, her ears heard something startling. Dishes crashed in the kitchen, followed by the shrill and panicked voice of her mother, yelling, "Mamma!"

Perry and his vapors disappeared, and Cecile ran into the kitchen. Paulina was face down, flat on the floor, and entirely motionless. Julia dropped to her knees and pulled her mother onto her lap.

Cecile had learned much from her medical reading, and she scolded sharply, "Mamma, don't move her. She might have a neck injury."

Julia ignored her and held her mother tightly. The scream had alerted the cousins. They arrived one at a time at the kitchen door to the outside.

Julia yelled out, "Someone call the doctor!" Then she turned with a frightening face to Cecile and ordered her, "Go sit on the couch and pray for your Mema!"

Cecile obeyed. She hurried to the couch, took the Rosary from the side table drawer, and began to pray. She stumbled through the well-known prayers. How could she concentrate? She strained her ears in worry, but nothing clear came through the door from the panicked clamor of voices in the kitchen — not for about twenty minutes, until a new voice joined the sounds, a calm, deep, full voice. The doctor had finally arrived from Cottonport.

His voice penetrated the others, and Cecile could hear him sending the cousins away. The doctor's voice was low and pure, and it carried through the walls. Cecile focused on every word, and on his tone, which did not sound worrisome. Within a few minutes, another voice found her ears, a wonderful voice.

She heard Paulina, "Caww, I don't know *what* happened. Oooh cher, the room is spinning."

There was some bustle in the kitchen, like the serving of coffee by a shaky waiter.

Paulina's voice came through stronger, "Oooh, that's bitter!" and after a short pause, she continued, "I'm better now, Dr. Perry. Now instead of two of you, I see only one."

At hearing the familiar name Perry, Cecile looked to the center of the floor, where Perry always appeared to her. It was just a floor. Her mind began frantically making connections, jumping from "what if" to "what if", until Paulina continued, "Julia, sugar, you remember Dr. Perry. Did you know he used to work for us when he was a boy. But, oooh, he's smart. He taught himself how to read and now look at him, coming to my rescue like an angel from Heaven."

Cecile held her breath through every word, scared to miss a single syllable. She heard Dr. Perry suggest they move Paulina into the living room, and Cecile's heart rose into her throat. The door opened, and a black gentleman in his early sixties walked through, supporting Paulina under her arm, with Julia on the other side of her. The doctor wore an elegant brown, pinstriped, three-piece suit. His hair was mostly gray, with speckles of its youthful brown scattered across the thinning top.

He and Julia helped Paulina to a chair against the adjacent wall. When Paulina was settled, she told him, "Doctor, this is my grandchild, Cecile."

At the mention of Cecile, Dr. Perry turned quickly to look at the couch. His face went blank and his mouth hung slightly open. His hands shook at his sides, as if from tremors. For the next fifteen seconds, aside from the doctor's trembling hands, the room was as still and quiet as a painting.

Perry's voice squeaked out, sounding much more like his adolescent self, "Cecile?"

Cecile leaned forward and gazed beyond the gray hair, through the wrinkles, and directly into his eyes. She squinted her focus more sharply. He had grown tall, and matured into a distinguished older gentleman, educated, accomplished, and respected. Upon realizing without any doubt that her ghostly friend stood before her as an old man, as real and solid as herself, she relaxed all of her features. She sat back. Her raised shoulders dropped. Her facial expression melted from one of intense scrutiny to the warm and pleasant look of a young Cajun lady welcoming an old friend into her house.

"Perry," she spoke with tenderness, "you are *not* a ghost. You *are* real. And you have legs, just as you said. It is nice to see you with legs."

Julia was mortified that her daughter would address the doctor so informally and speak to him with her strange ghost talk.

Perry, still shaking as if from chills, lit up with delight. His complexion blazed, as he answered, "And just as you said, you are *not* an angel. You *are* a girl. Here you are, just as I remember you. How is this happening?"

Julia, who had lowered her head into her hands, perked up at his remark. She dared to ask, "Doctor?... Do you know what she's talking about?"

"Of course I do," Perry answered through a continuing expression of astonishment, "I met her right here in 1909. She appeared to me for years, just like she is now, until she finally convinced me to go to school. And I never saw her again."

He raised his palm toward Cecile with a look of deep concentration, as he recalled fifty-year-old memories. He continued, "Only she was always clouded in green vapors, and she wasn't there." He raised his hand halfway up the wall and added, "She was there, floating."

Paulina, who had sat quietly in recovery, followed the exchange closely, and she corrected him, "No, Doctor, she was just as you see her now. It was you that was lower."

Julia closed her gaping mouth to say, "Mamma?"

Paulina sat up, very much recovered, and she explained, "I have heard of such things..., in this old house..., over the generations..., connections through time, special connections between special people. Well, this explains things. I had a feeling."

Cecile, sharp-witted as always, figured it out and announced, "The house was lower, wasn't it?"

Paulina clapped her hands and answered, "Yes, we raised it after the flood of '27."

Perry looked around him as his smile widened and memories continued to rush into him. "Yes, yes, it *has* been raised. I remember now. It used to stand on short red bricks." He looked down to his feet, then up to Cecile on the couch, as he calculated the measurements. "I would say about three and a half feet."

Paulina confirmed his estimation, "Yes, exactly."

Perry looked down to the floor again. When he returned his eyes to Cecile, her hand was stretched out toward him. She had been an angel to him, and he a ghost to her. They had taught each other, counseled each other, laughed and cried together, but there was one thing their friendship had always been without — physical contact. The room froze with anticipation for the following moment.

Perry reached his hand toward Cecile. She stood from the couch, took the one necessary step, and grabbed his hand. They stood like that for half a minute, squeezing the other's hand and staring into each other's eyes. A half-giggle, half-cry popped from Perry's nostrils. It was all the invitation Cecile needed. She lunged at him and threw her arms around his waist. He wrapped her tightly in an embrace. They squeezed each other, patted and rubbed each other, while Perry shook with uncontrollable sobs.

Under normal circumstances, the embrace would have been strange, but under the strange circumstances, the embrace was normal. It was right. It didn't matter that an older black man held a young white girl in such an affectionate hug. What should have been scandalous in the extreme was the most perfect moment the old farmhouse had ever witnessed. He had thought about her his whole life, for fifty years he believed her to be an angel, or some other Heavenly apparition sent by God to put him on the path of his life, and he had prayed daily to the angel who came to him when he was a child and befriended him, taught him how to read, and filled him with hope and ambition for a bigger life. She had seen him mere minutes earlier. They stood there not as an old black man and a young white girl, but as old, dear friends.

Julia had been holding her breath as she tried to make sense of the scene before her. She was an intelligent woman, but what her brain wrestled with that day was just beyond its abilities. She finally released her held breath, as her knees buckled beneath her. Paulina stood and assisted her daughter to a chair. Together, they watched — Julia in delirious confoundedness, Paulina in delight.

Perry and Cecile sat down together on the couch. He talked about the pisiform bone, and all the stories they had made up together that helped him through medical school. Perry's laugh had not changed. Oh it was deeper, and it bounced off the walls with bold manliness. But it was the same laugh Cecile had heard many times before.

As they talked, he never took his eyes from her face. He hadn't seen her in decades. For his many years she had been his deepest, most personal secret. He had struggled over the years to keep her image clear in his memory. Right then, with her face mere inches from his, it was like he had never forgotten.

Cecile had little to tell him about the months since she had visited him last. Perry, on the other hand, had a whole lifetime, an education, a career, a wife, children, grandchildren. She wanted to know it all, and coaxed him out of his hypnotizing wonder, begging him for answers.

Life had brought him many blessings. His lifelong gratitude to her was at the center of each. He thanked her profusely, using every term for thankfulness in his expansive vocabulary.

167

She interrupted him, "You make it sound so one-sided. You have changed my life."

"Corn husks and crowder peas?" he asked her, "That is nothing beside—"

"Is that what you think?" she blurted forth, "Is that what you have thought? You're right. Corn and peas are nothing. A friend like you is everything. You have changed the way I see the world, the way I see the people around me."

Julia slowly began to regain her wits, and she connected the surreal conversation before her with her daughter's unusual behavior all year. She thought about Christmas Mass as St. Augustine, and about gifting sand candles to protesters. In her dreamy state, she thought about how the changes in Cecile had changed the whole family. It began to make sense.

"She's right, doctor," Julia injected into the conversation, "Cecile changed last year. She changed us too, and now I know why."

"You see, Perry," Cecile continued, "you put beauty in my eyes, and now I see it where I never did before. Isn't that more than corn and peas?"

"And there's more," Julia added, turning to Cecile, "Dr. Perry saved your life. You were delivered by a midwife, and Dr. Perry came shortly after. You stopped breathing. You were turning blue, and I thought I was going to lose you. Dr. Perry took you from me, turned you and spun you. He held you upside down and struck you on the back. Then you started to cry. He saved my baby, but I didn't know he used to work on the farm."

Cecile held her breath as she listened. The revelations were overwhelming. She only released her breath when she looked at Perry and finally said, "You were right. You said it, and you were right."

"Right about what?" Perry asked.

She squinted her eyes at him and told him, "You said that you would save me, remember? You said 'When I become a doctor, I will pay you back. I will be *your* doctor, Cecile, and I will save you.' Do you remember?"

Perry's sobs began anew, and he answered between heavy breaths, "I remember, but I didn't know. I didn't know that baby was you, my angel, my Cecile."

He struggled to breathe as he sank into the depth of the revelation. It was a strange, delicate, and tender moment that belonged to only the two of them. Paulina excused herself and dragged Julia with her into the kitchen. They said very little to each other as they slowly prepared refreshments for their surprise guest and his childhood friend. What was there to say? The occasion was too big and too bizarre for words.

In the living room, words flowed more freely. The shock of the situation settled. The extreme emotions eventually subsided, and Perry and Cecile spoke as they always did. Then a word or gesture would touch Perry in a place he forgot was tender, and his emotions swelled again into heavy cries. As they reconnected on the couch, something was happening in Cecile's heart that she didn't know was happening. She was slowly uniting the Perry she had known with the one who sat beside her, the one holding her hand in his. Before she knew it, the love and friendship she held for the boy belonged entirely to the man. By the time Paulina called them into the kitchen for refreshments, Cecile saw Dr. Perry as her friend, the same friend in a different form, wiser, with a lifetime of experiences to share with her.

Oh, but it was better than before. Not only could she speak freely *to* him. She could speak openly *about* him. She could embrace him, feel his embrace in return, hold his hand, and above all, know that he would not disappear in green vapors.

As they finished refreshments, Paulina invited Dr. Perry to come back and visit as soon as he could.

"That's already arranged, Mema," Cecile said with a wink to Perry.

"Yes, Miss Paulie," Perry added, "I agreed to come by tomorrow…, to check on you and visit Cecile. My wife has passed and my children are long-grown, and I…, well…, we haven't seen each other in…"

"That's only half-true," Cecile reminded him, "I spent a month with you this summer."

"Yes, of course. I remember that month well. We danced."

Paulina remembered the dancing and knew at that moment that Perry had been there. Again feeling like the third wheel of a bicycle, she spoke up, "Dr. Perry, this house is as much your home as it ever was. You are always welcome."

Nobody noted the passage of time until the sun was touching the horizon. Perry excused himself, saying, "It's unlikely I'll sleep a wink tonight, but I should go home and try anyway. When I come back tomorrow, I'll bring pictures of my wife and children…, and my diaries. You'll see how I have thought of Cecile, how I called to her when I was in need, and how I never forgot her, even when I wasn't sure she was ever real."

They all saw Perry to the door. Each of them gave him a hug. Perry bent low to receive a kiss from Cecile through the thinning hair on his head. Cecile watched as he drove away, then joined her Mema at the kitchen table.

Chapter Twenty:
The Two Week Absence

AFTER DR. PERRY LEFT THE HOUSE, Julia served coffee to Paulina and Cecile in the living room, not to herself. It was all too much for her to grasp. She lay down in bed and silently reviewed everything she had just experienced.

Paulina was quite recovered, and she suggested they move to the kitchen, where they could speak openly without disturbing Julia.

Once they settled in the kitchen with their coffee, Cecile sternly asked, "Mema, why didn't you ever tell me about Perry?"

Paulina sipped her coffee and answered, "Honey, I told you about him."

"You did not!"

"I did. Dr. Perry is Poor Celeste's boy, the one who got the *good* job."

Cecile's head spun as she struggled to connect all she had heard about Poor Celeste with everything she knew about Perry. It was Poor Celeste whose husband was lynched in Shreveport. It was she who fled to Avoyelles Parish with baby Perry, and she who stayed and worked even after Dr. Perry got his good job. And Perry was the older gentleman they saw kneeling at her grave.

171

Once she made sense of it all in her own head, Cecile asked her Mema, "Did you know, Mema, that her husband was hanged by a mob?"

"Whose husband was hanged?"

"Poor Celeste. It was in Shreveport, when Perry was only a baby. That's why they came here. You see, you saved her. That's why she wouldn't leave you, even after her son became a doctor. And I bet Perry told her about his angel, the one who taught him to read. She was a woman of great faith. You said that, so she must have believed him. You said she was always grateful, and you didn't know why. Of course she wouldn't leave this house. She thought angels came here."

After telling her that, Cecile froze in place, all except her widening smile.

"What is it?" Paulina asked.

"Nothing. Just some irony, some beautiful irony. Perry's father was killed for trying to get a *good* job. I wonder what that mob would think of Perry if they could see him now."

"Well cher, times change."

"No Mema, times don't change. People change, or they don't change. In one year, I changed. Perry changed me completely, but all over the city, things stay the same."

"Well boo, if you're right, we can't wait for times to change. We better start changing people."

Cecile smiled so hard, her face hurt. She raised her coffee cup. Paulina did the same, and they clinked their cups together in agreement. They finished their coffee and said goodnight.

At the end of the tightest hug she had ever given her grandmother, Cecile asked, "So you really are Perry's Miss Paulie?"

"It appears that I am."

Cecile changed into her nightgown and made up her bed on the couch. Her thoughts were on Perry, but she wasn't awaiting the appearance of a ghostly boy, rather anticipating the visit of a real, flesh-and-bone friend, who she knew would be coming the next day.

Before the sun rose, every aunt, uncle, cousin, and neighbor in Avoyelles Parish was at Paulina's house. Word had spread of her collapse, and the stoves and ovens of the parish had been in full vigor all night, preparing food to bring to her. It was harvest time for all of them, but nothing was more important that day than Paulina. She had more food in her kitchen that morning than the old house had ever seen, and more hands working her fields. That is the Cajun way. They go where they are needed most, and they come together for each other like no other people in the world.

The hospital in Cottonport served the whole area, and Perry made house calls across the Parish. It is a good thing he did, and a good thing Paulina worked herself too hard in the hot sun. But Paulina was not the only one in need. Perry couldn't make it as agreed. He called the house and spoke to Cecile. She understood. He promised to come by the following day. Cecile was sad, but not for long. The sense of community on the farm was intoxicating. She met many new people, and reconnected with others.

At the end of the day, when all but the three ladies of the house had left, Cecile sat alone on the couch. It was the time and the place she would have waited to see green vapors. She thought of young Perry, but not as a friend she could see. She thought of him more as the youthful version of an older friend. It didn't occur to her to look for the boy Perry in his usual spot in the floorboards. She didn't look, and he didn't come. Perry was only the older gentleman who promised to visit the next day. It was with that thought that she fell asleep, and with that thought she awoke excited.

That next day was much calmer. The whole community was assured of Paulina's well-being, and they all returned to the concerns of their own households. It was a cooler day, and Julia and Paulina were in the field when Perry arrived. They saw him drive up, came to greet him, then returned to the work of the harvest.

Before they did, Paulina told Perry, "You were always good at the harvest, and now that you have a doctor's hands…"

"Mamma!" Julia shouted in embarrassment.

"I was just going to say," Paulina continued, "since he taught Cecile so much about the harvest, they might like to husk some corn together while they talk."

Cecile was giddy with the idea. There was one question that had burned in her since last harvest. Who could shell crowder peas faster? She challenged him. He accepted. And the two of them tore from the house with baskets.

They didn't count peas. They kept no time. Their hands shelled peas while they talked like old friends. As the afternoon aged, Perry offered to come back the next day and help with the corn.

Julia was still uneasy accepting the doctor's help, but he reminded her, "Miss Julia, as you know, my wife passed some time ago. After the funeral, I threw myself into my work. I haven't taken a vacation in years."

"You deserve a vacation, Doctor," she told him, "relaxing, not sweating on our farm."

He explained, "There's a reason I kept working. What else would I do? Where would I go on vacation? My children have their own lives, their own families and careers. I'm due for some time off and I'd like to spend it here, helping you and paying off an old debt."

Cecile slapped him on the shoulder. When he turned to her, she was looking at him with a very serious expression, as she told him in a soft voice, "There is no debt. I gave you hope and ambition. You gave me a beautiful world filled with beautiful people."

"You're right, Cecile," he acknowledged, "That was just an excuse, and a poor one at that. The truth is, I am drawn to be here, with you, of course with you, my old friend, but also here on this farm, with Miss Paulie and Miss Julia. I can't explain it, but I really want to be here."

Nobody had the words to argue with that, not even Julia. Perry came back the next several days and helped with the corn. When the corn was finished, he came to cut the sugar cane, then pick the tomatoes. He worked hard with them every day, and before long, they *all* loved him. But he was Cecile's first and foremost.

Perry spent two meals with them every day, either breakfast and dinner, or dinner and supper, depending on when he arrived. At the end of the day, two weeks after he first came to them, he sat alone in the living room with Cecile. He had brought his diaries from many decades earlier.

They were just as he said. His whole life he had thought of her as an angel, sent to him by God to put him on his path. Perry began keeping a diary in adulthood, but in them, he recounted all of his memories of Cecile, from their very first encounter.

He was reading to her from one of the entries from his mid-twenties, when he paused, and his smile went wider. "The pages," he whispered, "the folded pages. I had forgotten about them."

Cecile's eyes widened as revelation possessed her mind like an anxious spirit. Her eyes darted from side to side as she thought.

"Yes!" she finally spoke, "Of course! I turned to an unfolded page and asked you to fold it in your book. It *was* the same book. And when you folded it, it was folded in mine, and had been since 1910."

The mystery of the folded pages had been a minor agitation, but settling it once and for all was a joyful moment. Cecile leaned into Perry and squeezed him tightly. He held her head like it contained his very own heart.

Cecile was eager for more answers. She pulled herself from him and begged, "Go on. Read some more."

He read his youthful recollections of their summer of dancing, and of the time he spent waiting for her to return for the next harvest. Suddenly, in the middle of a word, he stopped cold. A puzzled look came over his face.

"Go on," she demanded, but he just stared at the page.

When she noticed he was holding his breath, she asked him, "Perry, what is it?"

He closed the old diary, rubbed his head as if it hurt, and raised his eyes to her, covering his mouth with his hand.

She demanded, "Tell me what it is!"

He lowered his hand and asked her in a shaking, faltering voice, "When was the last time you saw me?"

She gestured to him right in front of her.

"No, I mean the young me. When was the last time you saw me?"

"It was on our first day back here, the day my Mema fell. Why? What's wrong?"

Perry drew a slow and labored inhale, held it for several long seconds while staring deeply into Cecile's eyes, then released it, saying, "I have to leave here, and I can't come back."

"What do you mean," she begged him, "Where do you want to meet?"

"You don't understand. I can't see you anymore. I have to leave. I have to leave now and never see you."

The terrible announcement seemed to come from nowhere. Cecile shook her head, grinding her teeth together.

"I'm sorry, Cecile," he continued in a hoarse whisper, "You know how much I love you."

"No, no," she insisted between quick breaths, "This makes no sense. You want to be here. You said so."

"Yes, I want to be here…, with you, but I can't. I have to leave."

Cecile began crying, as she asked him, "Why?"

Perry patted his diary, as he told her, "There was a harvest, fall of 1910…, this fall. I knew you were coming. I waited for you. You appeared to me for a moment, came to me, bent low to kiss me, then disappeared. I didn't see you for two weeks. I didn't talk with you, read with you, make up stories with you. You were gone for two weeks…, **these** two weeks. Don't you see? I can either have you now or have you then…, and he needs you more than I do."

"No!" Cecile protested through her flowing tears.

"My dear, sweet friend, think of it. If I didn't have you then, if you didn't come back to me, I would never have gone to school, never become a doctor. I would never have met my wife, had my children, my grandchildren. I would never have helped the people I have helped. I would never have saved *you*! You see? I have to go."

"No," she continued to argue, "I will miss you too much."

"No, you won't. You will have me."

Cecile stopped crying, wiped her wet face, sniffed, and asked, "So, I came back to you?"

"You did. You finally came back after two weeks, and you were different."

"I was different?"

"Yes. You had been crying, and you looked at me with different eyes, more loving, more proud, more painful, yet more hopeful. Oh, Cecile, I wish I could tell you what you mean to me, what you have always meant to me."

Perry stood from the couch, bent over her, cupped her cheeks in his hands, and gave her a long kiss on the head. He drew a deep inhale, and released the kiss. He pulled away, still cupping her cheeks, looked at her with painful adoration, kissed her again, told her he loved her, and walked from the house.

Cecile followed him to the front door and watched as he got in his car and drove away. She stood in the doorway and cried. When her eyes finally went dry, she closed the door and returned to the living room. She stood and watched the green vapors appear.

Young Perry followed shortly behind, yelling, "Cecile, where have you—"

"Shhhh," she quieted him. She raised a finger to her lips, walked to him, and reached to touch him. When her hand passed through him, she winced in pain as she held her other hand to her heart.

She took up her medical book, sat on the couch, and told him, "We have work to do. I owe you that. I owe you everything."

He listened. He learned. They laughed. They made up new stories, and they continued on as they had been. But Dr. Perry had remembered well. There was something different about her and he noticed the difference the moment she shushed him. When Cecile came back to him, she had a new vision, penetrating in ways he would not understand for fifty years. They were still children. They were still friends, but when she came back after two weeks, she was even more like an angel.

Moving Forward

PERRY APPEARED TO CECILE FOR ANOTHER FOUR YEARS, until he went to school. It was 1914 for him, and he was seventeen years old. In those four years he learned from Cecile everything she learned in her school, and much more. Cecile never saw Dr. Perry again. He had intended to visit her after he knew his younger self had gone off to school. He didn't make it that long. He passed away. His heart stopped working, but its final beat was a joyous one.

Although he drove away from Cecile broken-hearted that day, he lived the rest of his days in peace and faith. He had been raised to be a faithful child, raised by Celeste to believe in God and Heaven. But like all the faithful, he doubted, that is, until he saw with his eyes and felt with his hands that the angel sent to him by God was real. He knew their connection was eternal and Heavenly, and he knew he would see her again.

As for Cecile, she continued making up stories long after she stopped seeing Perry. She wrote them down, and Perry was the co-author who resided in her heart. She published many books. Among them was the adventures and antics of a band of young blood cells and the angry old pisiform bone who always yelled at them for not helping on the farm.

www.ingramcontent.com/pod-product-compliance
Ingram Content Group UK Ltd.
Pitfield, Milton Keynes, MK11 3LW, UK
UKHW030842180225
455237UK00013B/154/J